BEASTS OF THE FIELD

ALEX

WEBB

WILSON

ISBN 979-8-9869462-6-9

Cover design by: Jaya Nicely
Printed in the United States of America
Library of Congress Control Number: 2023937342

Kelp Books, LLC

FOR LAURA

If you're not careful, the camera can turn into your eye,
the only dream you see through.

—Denis Johnson, *Tree of Smoke*

Part I

Landscapes

and

Portraits

The sicarios *crossed the border with the commuters from Tijuana. The two men were dressed in work boots and sweatshirts, identical to the laborers in the line of vehicles. They waited their turn to be inspected in the cab of the truck, holding black coffee to warm their hands against the chill of the dawn.*

They purchased pastries from a man beside the road and turned on the heater and ate in silence. They licked the sugar from their fingertips and watched as a yesaro *set out a selection of piggy banks—plaster mice in overalls, the Virgin Mary, a tortoise holding a signpost. Ahead in the road, a boy without legs began to juggle.*

When they reached the first checkpoint, they showed their papers and were waved into San Diego County. They switched cars in San Ysidro and continued north. In Los Angeles, they parked and waited for nightfall. When the light inside of the apartment on Pico was switched off, they sat for another hour, then closed the car doors silently and climbed the staircase to a landing.

They were in his bedroom before he could wake, and he made very little noise once they severed his trachea. They wrapped his ear in a page from an American magazine, then shot a Polaroid of him on the once-white sheets and mailed the package to his father.

1

IMAGES PASSED through his mind, photos he had taken and photos he imagined—a car burning in a broken street, a soldier kneeling in a field of poppies. The compositions shifted, one into another, as he lay in the unfamiliar house by the ocean.

When Robert Ellis opened his eyes, the glare from the window had reached across the bed. Around him the room hung dull and blue in the new day, the space chilled by the air conditioning. He watched as the previous night dissolved—fan blades spinning in a Central American airport, dirt roads through the jungle. He walked to the bathroom sink and splashed his face.

In the kitchen downstairs, a trail of ants stretched across the tiles. He stepped over the insects and went to a safe in the cupboard and ran the code he had programmed into the dial pad. His external hard drive sat against the back wall, along with his camera, his lenses, and his passport. The booklet was marked and faded, the most recent stamp in light-green ink, the seal of the República de Nicoya. He had been in the country for less than sixteen hours.

He moved the two lenses to the counter and unscrewed the sensor cover on the Mark III and attached his 200mm. Then he loaded the camera and the 50mm into a backpack and left the kitchen.

Outside, the morning was already bright, and the air smelled of the ocean, which lay in sight to the west beyond a field of sunburned hay. At the edges of the property, the rain forest had already begun to reclaim the line where it had been cut back. To the north and east the trees outlined a cove and climbed across a row of volcanic cliffs. A mile to the south, blurred in the heat, a river mouth joined the Pacific.

When he arrived at the beach house the previous night, the landscape had sat black under the moonless sky. He had found the lockbox in the dark and let himself inside, impatient simply to stop moving. Now he looked up at the saturated detail of the jungle as he crossed the clearing, the blades of dead grass rustling sharply under his feet.

A wasps' nest hung in the tree ahead of him, and he adjusted his course around it, ducking a final branch in the undergrowth to step onto the beach, where the undiluted sun baked the black sand, heat rising to meet heat.

He shifted the weight of the camera on his shoulders and set out toward the estuary, searching for photos as he walked, trying to remember how he used to be able to watch everything around him, studying the background behind people's faces, considering which elements should remain and which should be left out of a composition.

At twenty-eight, he was already exhausted by the sprawling parking lots of rental car agencies, the drained battery packs and laptop wires, the indifference of Manhattan's skyline each time he returned home from an assignment.

He had been sitting in his apartment in the East Village the day he realized his career was no longer in ascent. He had looked at his G5 hard drive, his color-calibrated monitor, his Canon lenses and Hasselblad, and admitted that he might be searching for some concept of success forever, and never find it—and that his editorial retainer would never compare to his father's income trading derivatives or to the income of some of his friends.

He was the youngest staff photographer on his masthead, and the people he grew up with continued to ask him if he was still living alone in Manhattan and if he was still shooting weddings. They didn't know or seem to care that his stock images were selling well through Getty and that one of his shots from Afghanistan had run as a cover in Europe.

He'd expected his work to eventually reach a place where those kinds of questions would end. Lately, he had begun to feel like that should have happened already. What he had not expected was to become detached in the way he had seen other photographers become detached, and to lose the ability to find why a photo, even technically perfect, was lifeless in the frame.

Near the north bank of the river, he stopped and reached for his camera. Ahead of him, two clumps of beach seemed to rise up and walk, and he was taken by this illusion, made watery by convection, until he realized it was a pair of feral puppies, awkward with youth and almost identical, moving on the sand.

The littermates slunk from a hole in the berm and circled something they were eating. He panned across their feet to the exposed eggs in a turtle nest, where a cloud of flies had gathered, suspended over the broken shells.

He photographed the dogs until they were finished, one chewing a flake of calcium, licking its muzzle as it wandered up the beach into the jungle.

·

The agent had said she was with the James Bell Gallery in Chelsea. Ellis sat across from her in a café near Union Square, where it was dark and her face was pale, lit by the screen of a tablet.

"I've never sold any of my work in bulk," he told her.

"I know your agent usually handles this, but my client wants to work with you directly," she said. "This is the offer he sent us this morning."

She pushed the tablet across the table and the blue light fell away from her face.

"He's putting together a private collection," she said. "He specifically told me how he saw your last feature in the magazine and fell in love with the portraiture. He's prepared to wire an advance today, and he wants to meet you."

"So he's not in the city?"

"At the price he's offering, I think it's worth it. We'll handle the arrangements."

"I just got back into town last week."

"I'll let you decide what you want to do, obviously," she said. "Only let's discuss the payment and the rest of the details first. My client's prepared to offer five thousand per photo. He wants to purchase every outtake from the Los Angeles portrait that made the magazine. So anything that didn't run last month, but just from that shoot. And if you retained the resale rights, he'll also pay double for the LA portrait that did get published."

"The magazine owns that photo," he said.

"Well," she said, "even without it, we're still talking significantly more than you'll ever see from editorial."

He'd connected from JFK to the Nicoyan capital of San Quintín, then to a pallid airport that stretched across a plain outside of a town named Iberia.

The beach house, six hours to the west, sat on the same property as the client's estate in the hills, where he was scheduled for an appointment at six.

•

He stood under the showerhead to wash off the sand and the heat and the vision of the puppies. An anole lizard hung from the wall near the ceiling, its translucent skin pressed to the tiles. In the florescent light, he could see its lungs pumping through the outline of its ribs.

He dried his body in front of a table fan in the bedroom and dressed, the pool in the yard shimmering through a window, sunlight running on its surface. He attached his laptop to the external hard drive at an island in the kitchen, highlighted a folder, and dropped it into Photoshop.

Images opened on-screen, RAW files shot digitally—cows in a wallow surrounded by wind turbines, two men having a conversation across a desk in a bank, the Ten Commandments hand-painted on a rock, a white Hula-Hoop in the center lane of a highway. He'd spent two months driving west from New York to capture them.

The feature had run as thirty-six images chosen from nearly four thousand. He'd sat with the photo editor for five nights to narrow the selection.

Now he scrolled forward, fast at first, then more carefully through the unedited bulk of the project. He opened a panoramic photo of Hollywood, a solitary oil field in the hills—rusted well pumps framing the lights of Sunset Boulevard—and moved backwards through the images, trying to orient himself chronologically. When he found the portraits the agent had described, he highlighted them and dropped them into a pane for editing.

The subject was looking away from the lens, his arms tattooed in blue-black ink, his face brown and smooth in the light of the hotboxes. The editors had run file number *090808042_LA* from this take.

He'd shot the photo, one of about fifty, toward the end of a twenty-minute session in an alley off La Cienega. The man had printed his name on a release in neat capitals along with his address, smiling a little as he wrote.

Two day later, Ellis had flown home to New York, completing the assignment.

·

Three hours passed at the island in the kitchen. He saved the portraits in a separate folder and finished correcting their color. He unpacked his camera and uploaded the shots of the puppies, then broke down the equipment and swam a few laps in the pool, his body loose and weak from the heat.

Upstairs he stripped out of his trunks and lay on top of the sheets and watched a television on the far end of the room, wrapped in a towel, flipping through the channels, listening to the pockets of Spanish. It was impossible for him to tell where the shows had originated—the telenovela girls Argentine, Panamanian, Colombian.

One of the actresses, by the angle of her head as she spoke, reminded him of Kara, his girlfriend—his ex-girlfriend, he corrected himself. He saw an image of her leg in a bed and remembered the photos she had emailed during the first week of her six-month assignment in Africa.

All of the movies on the other networks were American, a few with subtitles, most without. He watched a clip of the new president in the Rose Garden, his thin, dark face drawn after only five months in office. A graphic across the bottom of the screen contained text in Spanish about H1N1 vaccinations.

He shut off the television and closed his eyes, only to open them again. He tried to read a photography magazine from his backpack. Partway through a series of landscapes by Misrach, he fell asleep.

2

HULL RARELY dreamt. On most nights he would simply slip into a black river until he swam up onto its far bank in the morning, a vacant familiarity meeting him each time he closed his eyes. Occasionally, he revisited the ambush in La Libertad, but even this came to him less now. It had become harder for him to sleep as he aged, even with the ability to suppress his dreams.

He spent the siesta hours digging in his garden, sweating beside the guesthouse he had occupied for six months, while everyone but the guards rested within the walls of the jefe's compound. He was nearly finished, plucking and cutting in the afternoon light. He peeled a leaf from an oil palm that had contracted wither rot, and dried his gray hair with his sleeve.

At a cluster of crane flowers, he scanned for aphids, then extracted a tube of Honduran monocot and removed the snails he found, submerging them in a bucket of seawater at his side. Near the garden's north end, he paused above a sapling of American dogwood and recalled the smell of fall in Virginia, the soil of his first garden, cool and black, thousands of miles to the north. Then he returned to the same place he had found in his sleep, where he had learned to create a distance from nearly everything, including the grenade burst and the pain in his knees, which was old and settled instead of immediate and searing.

Whenever he allowed the civil war in El Salvador to skim into his thoughts, whenever it entered without his permission, he experienced the helpless terror that had overwhelmed him as he looked down at his ruined legs. Now he tried not to think about the war at all, or the pieces of himself that had disappeared in its wake. Instead, he focused on the garden and the sapling at his feet.

The bark on the transplanted tree had grown pale in the heat. Two of its buds had blossomed—the rest were dead—and below an axil, a thin line of mucus reflected the sunlight in rainbows.

A snail sat nearly motionless at the head of the secretion, touching the wood with the edge of its mouth.

He leaned forward from the neck and knelt, his knees throbbing, to pick it from the branch.

When his cell phone rang, he paused and looked down at the screen on his waist. Then he rechecked the snail's position and reached out and dropped it into the seawater, its shell striking softly against the tin at the bottom of the pail.

"*Ahuevo,*" he said.

"*El gringo sigue durmiendo.*"

"It's only four," he said. "The agent in New York told him six. If he's not awake in an hour, go inside and bring him up to the jefe. *Entiende?*"

"*Por supuesto.*"

The pain in his knees sharpened as he stood.

Carrying the bucket to a palapa, he dumped the water, pushing the mass from the bottom into one corner of a small sink. Then he scooped the bodies from the basin and flung them over the compound wall.

One slug hung in the razor wire for a moment before it dropped from sight with the rest. He avoided the dogwood tree and any thought of Virginia as he turned to leave the palapa. He showered in the cool shade of the guesthouse, rubbing the scars on his legs as the water traced across them.

3

THE DIRT road switchbacked into the hills, then ran under the trees like a tunnel. Ellis followed it for long enough that he stopped converting the kilometers to miles on the odometer.

When he finally reached the end, he braked beside the wall of a compound and checked the rearview mirror as three armed men came down from a guardhouse. They were dressed in suits despite the heat, each carrying some version of a Kalashnikov. He looked away from the muzzles, up at the darkening sky.

In his mind he saw the poppy grove in Afghanistan—his hands shaking as he framed an armored convoy. The closeness of the rifles now, just outside his window, kept him from taking the car out of neutral, even though he felt the same movement of fear and adrenaline in his fingers.

Two of the men stood twenty feet from the windshield, the magazines on their weapons taped end-to-end, flecks of silver on the barrels where the paint had been chipped. The third advanced in the flat, green light under the trees.

"*Buenas noches,*" he said, craning his neck to look inside the vehicle.

"*Esto es un hacienda de Janvion Garcia?*"

"*Uno momento,*" the guard said, and they waited.

Then one of the other men, near the wall, touched the wire in his ear and spoke something into his sleeve, and the guard beside his car also touched an ear and nodded and motioned for him to proceed.

As they stepped out of the road, Ellis left the engine in idle, then rolled through the gate, allowing the car to climb in first gear to the east. At a fork, he hesitated and turned, almost reluctantly, into the most obvious track, deeper into the jungle.

A feeling of elevation came to him as he continued, the mountainside dropping away through the trees to reveal a town below him, where pangas sat in small black rows on the sand, the upturned hulls still wet, shining in the lights from the shacks along the coast.

He braked for a smaller guard post at the rim of the overlook and parked among a mud-spattered Toyota Prado, a black Range Rover, and two off-road quads. Past the trucks, a cell tower stood at the edge of a buttress, affixed with transmission dishes.

A man came down from a blockhouse at the foot of the array and waited for him to exit the vehicle.

He seemed to be about sixty-five, and American, but it was hard to tell.

He was tall and gray and wiry and leaned forward from his neck.

"The jefe's waiting inside," he said, and Ellis checked for the weight of the hard drive in his pocket.

"I'm Robert," Ellis said.

"My name is Hull."

They climbed a stone staircase and entered a terra-cotta courtyard, where the annexes of the hacienda were arranged around a central fountain. A red bird flickered onto the highest tier and dipped toward the water, drinking, shook its wings, and dove off into the forest.

At an inner wall, Hull punched a keypad and directed Ellis inside of the building. They passed through a stock room and a modern kitchen, which was filled with women and stainless steel and more armed men, who stood placidly under the low ceilings and the steam from the pans, which smelled of meat and onions.

In the next hallway, they stopped in front of a set of red-stained doors, and Hull listened for a moment before he knocked. Then he turned the knob and allowed Ellis to enter ahead of him.

The office was so cold inside that condensation had formed on the windows.

A colonnade stood beyond the panes—the jungle and the hills and the ocean below, now almost black.

The jefe sat waiting behind a desk in a pair of shorts and a stained T-shirt.

As Ellis came forward, he rose and reached into his pocket and withdrew a small plastic bottle and palmed it.

"*Buenas,*" the jefe said, and stepped, barefoot, to the center of the room and unscrewed the cap and applied three drops of solution to each eye, pinching his nostrils. "I would have been happy to arrange for a man to pick you up at the airport. Did you have any trouble with the directions? I can have something brought up if you are hungry."

"No, thank you," Ellis said.

"Do you want something to drink?"

"I'm fine. I brought this hard drive to transfer the images."

"I am glad that you agreed to come to meet us," the jefe said, blinking. "I don't know how much Ms. White has told you, and we can talk about the payment if you would like. Maybe first, however, we can see what you've brought—the portraits from Los Angeles."

He gestured to a flat-screen monitor on the wall above his head, and Ellis handed him the hard drive. The jefe turned it over, its silver veneer reflecting the light, then sat back down, attached it to the computer, and opened the photos, ignoring the wall display as he scrolled through the portraits, focusing instead on the desktop screen in front of him, pausing occasionally to study something of interest.

Overhead, Ellis saw that he had adjusted the contrast in the images so that the light falling on the alley and the subject were bluer now than they had been in the uncorrected RAW files, which was how the jungle looked beyond the windows.

"You know," the jefe said after a moment, "these pictures capture my son perfectly. I advised him, when he moved to Los Angeles, that the Zetas are very hard to track, and that to compete with them, you have to be very hard to track as well. Not here, so much. Here, you are safe." He inclined his head toward Hull in the corner and pushed air though his nostrils.

Ellis looked over his shoulder, then back at the screen, where it was clear the subject had his father's eyes and cheekbones.

"Mr. Hull is very involved in this," the jefe continued. "Elsewhere, however, you need to be very careful, and my son should have known to never pose for these portraits. They are very nice. Did he just volunteer for them? That would be very much like him. He loved his tattoos, and he loved himself in many ways—they sent me a piece of him wrapped in a page from your magazine, the Zetas, did you know this? I can show it to you if you want." His voice became lighter, like a song. "What do you think? The caption, that is the term, contained his name and the street he lived next to in Los Angeles. Did he just give you that information? Did you just ask for it?"

Ellis stared at the image as the rest of the room narrowed to contain only the monitor, and tried to remember what they'd discussed while he was shooting, and how he'd decided to pick this face at the magazine with the editors.

"He looked like you," Ellis said, and it occurred to him that he hadn't called his father or any of the editors at the magazine in a very long time—or told anyone he was flying to Nicoya. He hadn't called Kara, who at one point had also begun to feel like home, in even longer.

A row of phone banks came into his memory from the terminal in JFK, the hard lines removed—a stewardess on a cell phone, leaning against a plastic divider. She appeared tired, the lines of her face softening only when someone picked up and she began to speak.

He also remembered explaining to his own father once, over the phone from an airport in Brazil, how his photography was changing and why he no longer photographed the sunrise and certain people whose beauty was too obvious. He had been traveling for so long by then that he was starting to feel homeless.

Then he remembered that in the alley he and the jefe's son spent a few minutes discussing his drive across the country, and the yellow grass in Kansas, and how neither of them had lived more than ten miles from the ocean. They were almost the same height and almost the same age and were wearing almost the same sneakers. They'd talked about a girl they'd both watched walk up La Cienega.

"He looked like you," he said again, and turned toward Hull, who was still leaning forward, almost painfully from his neck, then back toward the jefe. "All I know is that he looked like you. And that I want to go home."

The jefe picked up his eyedropper and unscrewed the cap, only to set it back down without applying the saline. Then he slumped in his chair and began clicking through the entire contents of the external hard drive: *DaiChopan_ Afghanistan. Ledger_LA. Breadth_USA. Recession_SanFran. NikeCampaign_Brazil. Fishermen_Durban.*

"What is this?" the jefe asked, and opened the first photo in the folder labeled *Pitbulls_Nicoya.* "Don't look so worried," he added. "I would just like to have a conversation. I was going to ask about your family, and your father and his house on Long Island, and maybe your girlfriend—she is also a photographer, and she is now in Marrakesh, if I'm not mistaken. I have a feeling you don't want to talk about them, however—it is difficult to discuss the people who are important.

"I thought, when I arranged for this meeting, that you might be working for my competition in some way, except now I can see that you are only a journalist. You would not have come if you were working for the Zetas, and if you did not come, that would have also told me something. It would have told me how to handle your people, though that is not necessary, so I will pay you for your photos. I am assuming you would like the money in the same account we used for the deposit. I also think I have something for you—some more work, potentially. Then maybe you can still make that flight home to New York, like you were planning."

On the monitor, the puppies stalked forward, low to the rim of the turtle nest.

The jefe's eyes seemed dry and were very bloodshot. He scrolled through a series of the pair eating and blinked, a motion more deliberate than instinctual.

"You know," he said, "these animals, they are only part pit terrier, I think, so you mislabeled them. If you took these photos at my river, I'm familiar with the man who bred them. I am surprised he didn't use these *cachorros* to bait his animals in training, since he has no eye for mixed breeding. Either way, ultimately, it would be very much like him to let them go and to not to see their potential."

4

THE JEFE spoke of the aristocracy in Europe, of how the rich once used canines to fight bulls. The practice, he said, went back to the Romans, who pitted beast against beast for sport, as they did with men.

"They fought in the Colosseum," he said. "Did you know this? Against bulls and bears. It is even written that a pack could take down a wild elephant."

The Range Rover swayed in the dark, and he leaned forward from the back seat, where he sat beside Hull, in order to speak directly into Ellis's ear.

"My father taught me these things when I was a boy in León," he said, and nodded toward the distant Caribbean, where he claimed to have been raised by the descendants of slaves and conquistadors and Chorotegas.

Ellis watched the jefe's face in the rearview mirror as the truck rocked over a pothole.

His father, the jefe explained, was a rarity for León—a man who bred mongrels which would never quit, no matter how exhausted or savaged. He had learned some of his technique in Honduras, where pit fighting was legal, and taught himself the rest, earning enough with his skill to send his children to a prep school in Panama, then on to college in the US, where the jefe had found access to people and wealth, the resources that had allowed him to build his empire.

"When I was a child," he said, "they would pay for my father's animals. People from all parts of the world knew his reputation. In León, our dogs would always win, and we would go to Honduras and win there, too, and they would come and ask him after each event, 'How did you do this?' and he would tell them, 'Nothing is for free, you must pay for my knowledge.' He worked with a man from Japan once, who came all the way from Kochi to breed a Tosa inu with a special fila Brasileiro that belonged to my family. It was very exciting.

"He grew up with a floor made of clay. But he knew enough to know that his dogs could buy us almost anything, and he always meant for me to receive an education. He said I could go to study in America for four years, to be enrolled with the sons of rich men, and that I would come back with everything we would need going forward. So I went and I met Colombians and Argentines, Brazilians, Russians, and Arabs. Americans, too, of course, it was a very good school, but the Americans were not as interested in the things my father and I found important.

"The dogs now," he said, and shrugged, "they are just as much a part of me as my father, so I cannot stop, even though he is gone, and even though we are transnational in most aspects and it is hardly worth the money."

He made the sign of the cross, then went on with more history, telling Ellis of terriers and the new pit bull breeds that some had crossed with mastiffs. He spoke of other bloodlines and combat dogs from Briton, which once tore their Roman counterparts to pieces.

"For seven years on the battlefields," he said, "when the Romans invaded in AD forty-three."

The animals were crossbred afterward, he continued, the conquerors enhanced by the conquered, the games at the Colosseum following, which led to baiting events across the Channel and the spliced genesis of the bulldog as the Roman Empire waned.

Developed to wrangle and tenderize wild cattle for butchers, the bulldog possessed admirable traits—squat and strong, vicious, loyal, and brave. These assets allowed it to stand against the bulls, which were adorned in flowers and bright-colored streamers of papier-mâché and paraded into amphitheaters, then fastened to a post, where they were pitted against speed and cunning, fortunes riding on the results in the ring.

"They would hold the nose," the jefe said, "where the bull is most vulnerable. They would wait for a man to come and secure a rope around the neck of the cattle. There's a story of an old bitch, which my father told to me. He said he heard it many times from older men, who heard it from men who were even older than they were.

"She possessed very good pedigree and was intelligent and brave, but crippled from a lifetime of fights when her owner brought her to a bait just after she'd given birth to a litter sometime around the year 1825. She was still nursing at the time, they say. She had pinned more bulls in her lifetime than dogs twice her size, according to the story, but there was one that she slept with in the barn on the owner's farm, and they were friends, and they were playful and gentle with one another, but in the ring they were enemies, and each bore the scars of the other.

"This bull in particular was known throughout the country for his madness, and he'd spent the afternoon that day goring other dogs. They say he had killed more than ten animals, I believe, when the bitch was released in the ring, so he had put together quite an effort and thus was bleeding from many places and getting much slower.

"According to how I have heard the story, she merely circled him at first, blind in one eye, limping and waiting, using her intelligence. Then when another dog was thrown, she moved to the bull's nose from his withers and pinned him, and the crowd appreciated this triumph, of course, where so many others had failed, so they paid their respects to the breeder with an ovation. Unfortunately, the animals also fell very hard, my father said, in a tangle, and when the men in the ring finally pulled them apart, the bull was finished."

"What happened to the bull, jefe?" the driver asked in a way that made it clear he'd already heard this story, and the jefe's reflection smiled, his face lit red by the brake lights.

"The owner himself put him out of his suffering, and he was butchered for a feast."

"And what about *la brava*, jefe?"

"The bitch was alive," the jefe said, "even though the bull fell with the weight of his head on her as she clung underneath. She was injured, but she could have lived for the rest of her life in the barn, though it would have been quiet for her. Her owner, however, was, among many other things, a salesman, so took her and stood her up beside the body of her old friend, who was now vanquished, and he cut her to pieces in front of the crowd with a razor to prove her pedigree and to show them the loyalty in her blood. And she allowed this. She didn't release the bull's face, even after she drew her last breath. They say he made enough to buy another farm, the parcel next to his, on the price of her puppies."

•

They rode in silence then, with only the sound of the engine and Hull shifting his legs, gravel ricocheting across the underside of the truck. After what seemed like a very long time, the Range Rover entered a clearing, and Ellis leaned forward to look up at a shape in the dark, which rose white and massive across the next valley—pale, curved slabs standing against the sky, the walls of a coliseum.

"Here we are," the jefe said. "I also know how to expand my holdings."

His current property, he claimed, covered seven times more land than his last estate and stretched across twenty-six square kilometers of rainforest.

He had purchased the parcel in 2005, after the second coup d'état in the capital, when he moved from the Caribbean to the Pacific coast of Nicoya. He'd built his compound at the top of the hill in less than a year, along with the assorted buildings that dotted the valley to the east, hiring every man from the town and working them in shifts until the hacienda and its satellites were complete.

The beach house, he said, which he'd never slept in, was the final building to be constructed, and when it was finished, he'd paid the townsmen more than they would have earned in a decade, and invited them to bring any animal they owned and may be comfortable parting with to the arena.

As Ellis climbed out of the truck, still staring up at the walls, Hull came to stand behind him. The jungle sat black beyond the headlights, and there was almost no wind this far inland. He noticed for the first time that the jefe was carrying a pistol in his waistband and that the other American seemed to always be repositioned just outside of his vision.

He could smell the dirt at his feet. He glanced down and saw that he was standing next to a puddle.

If they shot him from behind, he thought, his body would probably fall face-first into the water. He saw an image of a woman he had photographed beside the FDR, just north of Fourteenth Street, who had been found faceup, her arm pressed under her back, her skin pale and bloated from the river.

He wondered now if his father would be able to identify him if they found him outside of the arena. He told himself someone from the magazine would also probably call Kara, since they knew a few of the same people. He looked back at the puddle and watched the water. Maybe, he thought, she would save the unedited photos on the G5 in his apartment, if any of his work seemed worth saving.

When he met her, they'd both been drinking bourbon at a bar in the West Village. They spent maybe an hour talking about the people they knew and how they got into photography to begin with.

"I really like film," he said to her.

"That's like saying you like food."

"I guess."

"Or air."

"Or water."

"Totally," she said, and touched his arm. "What do you like about it?"

"I don't know," he said. "It's just that it's almost like a meditative process. It starts before you even pick up the camera. You have to choose how you want to depict the moment and intentionally select the right format. It simplifies everything."

She laughed and chewed on the ice from the bottom of her glass.

"It's not like digital," he said, "where you can just adjust everything afterward—where the image is so sharp and editable, if you're underexposed a half stop, you just bump it up a half stop, and everything is perfect. I mean, what's real? Is that even real?"

"It's not real," she said. "I need to shoot more with this Pentax I have in my apartment."

"I do, too, with my medium format. I have a Hasselblad and I hardly ever use it. It's like, are zeros and ones real? I know silver halide emulsion is real. You develop the film and it's like, this is what I did. It's tangible. But if you go on a shoot and you have thirty gigs of information that you have to download, all of a sudden you're more of a computer guy than a photographer. It's even worse when you travel."

"And when everyone's having dinner," she said, "or out partying, or whatever, you're sitting at your laptop, and it breaks the whole dynamic."

"How can you see what you're supposed to see if you're too busy staring at a monitor? I don't know. Look at the lineage—what if someone like Roberto Salas had been able to just show Che and Castro every image he'd shot of them?"

"They'd have known right away how he saw them," she said, "or whatever."

"Totally. It would have changed the way they behaved, especially in front of him. They would've known exactly what he was thinking. They'd have been able to see right through his work, which would've changed their perceptions of him and maybe changed his access. Then, who knows, we might've never seen that shot of Che leaning in when Fidel's lighting his cigar. It's like, what if that first take from Richard Avedon's Western series had been posted online right after he shot it?"

"Yeah," she said. "You know, I think I've figured out that I need to think more when I'm shooting. I shoot a lot by feel, and I get this amazing aesthetic with my single images. I just love them sometimes. Then when I think about shooting more for—when I think less about style, or focus on it less anyway, I make my editors happier. I need to start thinking about why I'm taking a photo and focus on sequencing and editing and narrative."

"I don't think you should change the way you shoot for your editors."

"I'm not talking about changing just to change for other people. I'm talking about getting better."

"I just think they haven't thought about it the way you have."

"That's kind of the point."

"Or they don't see things the way you do. They've spent five minutes thinking about something, and you've been thinking about it for weeks. They ask you to change something, and it changes everything. Sometimes I see things, but I can't get the photo, so I have to hold on to them and wait for them to happen again and be prepared for when they do, and that can take forever. Sometimes I can never get things the way I want them."

"Do you know what I miss the most about your country?" the jefe asked him.

He had walked around the truck and passed through the headlights. The insects and the frogs in the jungle became silent as his shadow stretched across the trees.

He turned his hands from palm up to palm down.

"The weather," he said. "The seasons. Here we have the rainy season and the dry season, and that's all and it's always hot, and even when it rains, there is sun most of the day in those months. In America you have the snow and the leaves that change colors in the fall. I liked to see that when I was in school. I liked the way the sun becomes thin there in the winter. The variety seems to be very American, even if it does get very cold."

"I don't know," Ellis said, and watched as the jefe's smile faded.

Then they all left the side of the Range Rover, and he stepped around the puddle.

They moved as a group to the wall of the coliseum, where a surveillance camera was mounted.

The jefe paused at a rusted steel door and depressed a buzzer with his ring finger, looking up into the camera. Soon a man unlocked the bolt from the inside, his face smooth and wide with hooded eyelids.

He wore a rubber apron and rubber gloves and made a bow with his head to the jefe, who touched him on the shoulder. He stepped aside and motioned them into the building and locked the bolt behind them.

"*Buenas*, Emilio," the jefe said, and filed past him down the hallway toward a room lined with kennels, the concrete echoing with the voices of barking dogs.

Water lay in puddles along the slab under the building, reflecting the light from the bulbs in the ceiling.

Ellis smelled the animals before he saw them, and tried to step back into the hallway, but the jefe intercepted him and guided him into the center of the room where, in a hollow sunk into the floor, a pit bull shot to the end of its chain and reared back, lowering its hips, then sprang forward again, snarling and running its tongue between its incisors, straining on two legs, gagging silently from the tension on its collar.

As the jefe edged him closer to the pit, he could also see a rooster, which was scrabbling along the walls, just out of the dog's reach, its wings clipped, the tips of its bones showing in flashes.

"This one is scatter bred," the jefe said. "I can't tell you what is in his blood, exactly. I know there is some American pit terrier and some Argentine mastiff and maybe a little bully kutta. Look at his size. He is not even fully grown, and Emilio tells me he already weighs sixty-eight kilos. We have been baiting him each day. He was very timid at first. He did not understand what we wanted from him or what was expected, but I think Emilio has fixed this."

He applied the saline, his eyes blinking and sliding back and forth, and said something in Spanish. He reached into a bucket and pressed a portion of dried beef into Ellis's palm, gesturing toward the animal.

"You can see he is hungry," he said. "You should attempt to feed him. It is interesting the first time you witness a dog baiting. We all require nutrition. I am just making that necessity into something he can use in the pit, a behavior which will serve a purpose."

Ellis took the jerky and saw a moment from a documentary in his mind—a water buffalo unable to stand, struggling to raise its head while jackals bunched at its midsection.

He remembered wondering what the cameraman might have been thinking, standing apart to shoot the footage. He had felt a sensation like heat in his neck while the water buffalo gently set its head on the ground, its pupils rolling back, its tongue lolling.

As he watched, the rooster moved into a corner of the pit and attempted to climb the walls, trailing feathers and small, bright drops of blood, kicking back at the dog with its spurs, the remains of its wings flapping in terror. Then Emilio relaxed the chains, and the dog took the bird, and Ellis was transfixed by the puffs of down, which were almost beautiful, swirling above the concrete. Once it was over, he slipped the meat into his pocket and followed the jefe, who was already disinterested and drifting toward the mouth of the tunnel.

5

IT WAS AFTER midnight when they climbed out of the training pits into the arena, the weight of an impending thunderstorm now pressing the starless sky. Ellis followed the jefe from the wings of the building and stopped beside him in the center of the *ruedo*.

"What do you think?" the jefe asked, and glanced back at Hull and the driver, who were watching them from across the empty ring.

"I don't know," Ellis said.

"You don't seem to know a lot of things. This is a common answer for you when I ask a question."

"I mean, I don't know what to say. I've never been anywhere like this. I don't really know anyone who has."

"I wouldn't think so," the jefe said. "This is not a place people you know would come to visit. We have a beautiful coastline, but this is not like the tourist locations of Nicoya. And we have a war—well, I still have a war. The new government doesn't have much to fight against anymore. They have made a deal with the rebels. But our wars have never been anything like what your last president made in Iraq. Our wars are always very small, and my war is very quiet, and there are no Americans here, except of course for Mr. Hull, only he is very good at making sure it is like he is not here."

"I'm an American."

"This is true. Maybe you're not here either."

"That's something else I don't know how to feel about."

"I have something for you to know. Five years ago, while I was standing over the blueprints for this building, I asked for a ring large enough to accommodate a corrida. And twice, when it was completed, I brought in matadors and bulls from the capital. I've also fought the dogs every week here, in a pit at the center of the ruedo. I know this place and my animals, and I have respect for what I've learned from my father. Do you understand this? Do you see what I'm trying to explain to you?"

"I don't think so."

"So then maybe we should talk about your life, then? This may illuminate things. I studied photography in school. Did you know this? I'm sure you couldn't. I didn't mention it. My instructor—it was my final year, I did not take it seriously—he told me to see things as they were and to capture them."

"I was just thinking something similar."

"It was only one class," the jefe said. "Tell me, why do you do what you do for a living?"

"I still don't know how to answer."

"You can try by listening to my questions."

"My dad gave me a Nikon when I was little."

"And did you study it in school?"

"Yeah."

"Where did you attend?"

"Visual Arts."

"In New York," the jefe said. "Four years, correct?"

"Yeah."

"And you get paid well for this?"

"Not exactly."

"So that's why you are here."

"I guess so."

"I haven't seen much of your work, only what you've showed me, but I think you see things like my professor explained. You must know what I mean. Americans like to talk about work."

"I don't know if I'm like other Americans."

"You don't seem very different in my opinion."

"I know I'm like other photographers. We look for photos. There are images everywhere. You just have to see them."

"And you can do this?"

"I guess part of me has always done it without even thinking. I didn't even know what a lot of it was called until I went to school. It's weird to hear something you've always done described by a teacher and realize there's actually a name for it—a technique, or whatever."

"And this is why you like it?"

"I think I like it because I'm good at it."

"There must be something else."

"I mean, there are a lot of things I like about it."

"With the animals," the jefe said, "for me, there is only one thing. It is about being close to the memory of my father. I suppose there is also something important about being close to them in these moments. What is more important than life when you can see something is so close to death."

Ellis looked into the jefe's bloodshot eyes and wiped his mouth, his saliva dense like caulk. He saw the rooster in the pits, followed by the puppies on the beach.

"Did your instructor ever tell you about *The Decisive Moment*?" Ellis asked. "Henri Cartier-Bresson?"

"I remember this name," the jefe said, and squinted. "He took portraits, I believe, if I'm not mistaken. Tell me more about him."

"He was kind of the father of modern photojournalism," Ellis said. "He worked from, like, the 1930s to the 1960s and shot all kinds of wars and Gandhi's funeral, some royalty. But if you leave out all the history and the famous people he photographed, what he really shot was life, just windows into people."

The jefe was smiling now, pulling at his lower lip and tapping his foot lightly in the dust.

"He published this book of photos," Ellis continued. "Most of it was street photography, like a guy jumping over a puddle, but shot in a way that really made you feel that this moment he'd shot was *the* moment. That jumping over a puddle was profound and pivotal in his subject's life, like it was more than just a photo."

"What was the name of this collection?"

"It was called *The Decisive Moment*. In the intro he talked about looking for that. He said something about how there's nothing in this world that doesn't have a decisive moment. And he said a photographer's job was to recognize it and know when to press the shutter button, to know when to take a photo. And he said that if you miss the decisive moment, the moment that's the visual representation of the essence of something, it's gone forever."

"This sounds like what I am describing," the jefe said, and nodded, bouncing on the balls of his feet. "I remember this man. He shot in black and white?"

"Yeah," Ellis said.

"I never liked his work. To me, it seemed, what is the word? It seemed exploitative. It seemed like he was using the people he took pictures of. He didn't stop to help those people plant their rice paddies?"

"That wasn't his job."

"So you are saying someone should only do his job?" the jefe asked. "That is very American."

"No. I mean, I just look at his work, and I think he was put here for something else. He was put here to take photos. When I shoot sometimes, I have to remind myself that the people I'm framing have entire lives that I can't see, and that they're real. It's the mind behind the instrument that produces the results. I heard that somewhere, and it's always something I think about. So I think about all the walking he must have done and all the life he must have rubbed up against to find those little courtyards in Europe, and those political rallies in Iowa, and the people in Turkey and China. They were so far removed from where he was coming from, or his experiences, and they were so far removed from his experiences, so he must have spent a lifetime exposing himself to life, capturing it and getting it under his skin, or whatever."

"And is that what you are doing here? Are you here to get something under your skin?"

"No," Ellis said. "I'm not here on an assignment."

"You are here to take my money," the jefe said, and unscrewed the cap on the saline dropper. "Please, though, finish with Bresson. Tell me, did anyone other than him profit from his work?"

"I guess his photos feel like he was interested in people. I think that's what you said. Maybe I said it. He was French, but he didn't just shoot France. And I think he did change things. He was shooting to make his viewer more aware of lives unlike theirs. He wanted to make people see places they'd never been and to understand them. And I think his work achieved that because street photography was so new then. It was sort of pure. The subjects didn't pose. They just did what they did and didn't think about the camera like people do now. They didn't think about the results. And the viewer didn't have as much exposure to images like his, or cynicism, or maybe as much sophistication, because the technology was still new, so they came to it from a more open prospective. So I don't know. I don't know if that's exploitative or if it's just human and intimate."

The jefe touched him on the shoulder as if Ellis had made some point for him.

"You know," the jefe said, "I think you are trying to defend things from the perspective you understand most clearly. I've had people here every Friday for almost five years, since I moved to this place. And they bring their animals, and I watch them against mine. There's actually a boy with a talent for the dogs in town. I'm going to hire him to help old Emilio in the pits. Now, I will ask you if you know about somebody. Did you ever study the life of Simón Bolívar in your schools?"

"I've heard the name, but I don't really know anything about him."

"He was a very great man in Latin America. He was a liberator, and he worked so the people in South and Central America could have their independence. He wanted, they say, to make a United States of South America, from here all the way to Patagonia and Tierra del Fuego. I think about his goal sometimes, and why he failed and the yanquis did not, and I think it has to do with his inability to think like they do. He had a certain type of will, but maybe the men in the US, they had more, and maybe they were more willing to overlook certain consequences, but that is beside the point.

"The thing I was going to say was that when he died, he asked his friend to destroy all of his papers, whatever he found of his writings and his letters. Yet his friend did not do this. He disobeyed Bolívar's wish from his death-bed, you understand this? He understood it is important to have a record. This is why I am saying I want you to see it tomorrow night. I want you to record my fights. There are many decisive moments here I think," he said, and something splattered into the dust at Ellis's feet. "I think it will help you to understand things in a way you've never considered."

It began to rain, and they crossed into the tunnel and climbed into the Range Rover.

6

HULL ADJUSTED his legs in the back seat and turned to watch the shadow hunched in the rain, standing at the door to the beach house. Then the photographer disappeared into the kitchen, and he tapped the driver, and the truck began to climb toward the hacienda.

They stopped again farther up the road, where a stream crossed the track, and shifted into four-wheel drive. Below the first checkpoint, they passed his men in the Prado coming back down the hillside.

"Padaratz lands in the afternoon tomorrow at the airport in Iberia," the jefe said over the sound of the rain. "I have the manifest. I would like you to pick him up and escort us to the arena."

"I think we should talk about the photographer," Hull said, and the jefe closed his eyes and leaned back in the seat.

He took the saline dropper from his pocket and squeezed it, moving his head in rhythm with the truck to pool the liquid in the corners of his eyes. The leather creaked beneath him.

"Alright," he said. "Tomorrow night, after the fights, please take his camera and dispose of him in the ocean. I would like you to keep your men on him until this moment."

"I'd prefer to do it tonight," Hull said. "If that's an option."

It had been eight years since he had killed another human.

After the government doctors had rolled him out of the Special Activities Division on disability at half pay and his 401K had disappeared in the recession, Hull knew he was going to have to return to a place like this.

He also knew he was going to lose his house in Virginia, which had been repossessed before he even contacted his source in San Quintín, looking for a solution. Now he wanted to believe that he could make enough money from the jefe to buy it back—or to find a replacement.

"What did you say?" the jefe asked.

"I said I'd prefer to do it tonight, if possible."

"What is the problem?"

"I might not have enough men tomorrow."

"How many men have you hired since you began? You have more than twenty. It is more like thirty if you count those two *técnicos* I'm paying from Los Estados. I'm paying them for three more guards or drivers if I wanted them."

"I haven't had enough time to work with them."

"Pay them whatever you like. You can trust them."

"It's not about the money. They haven't been through enough training."

"They can learn quickly," the jefe said. "It is your role to train them.

Listen to me. You worry too much. And I know that I pay you to worry too much, but I still think it is bad for you."

"I'd just prefer to do it tonight. The Prado's already back down at the beach house. We just passed it. Everything's in position."

"I know what you will say. I know what you are thinking: 'It should have been done already,'" the jefe said, slowing his cadence to imitate Hull's. "You are very practical. However, I also like this photographer. You heard what he said about capturing the essence of things. Well, he was right tonight, I think. In those photos of my son, I saw a weakness that I had never seen before in the blood of my own flesh. And also with the puppies? The pictures on his hard drive, with the eggs? Anything to survive. Good pedigree."

"If you like him, we should let him go."

The jefe rubbed his hands together and said something quietly in Spanish that Hull couldn't hear over the storm.

"I also like the point I am planning on making to him, and the message we might send through him. I don't expect you to see these things. We are still getting to know each other. The Mexicans, they know this, however. They know this better than anyone. Do you know in Tijuana last week they found the head of a reporter who was just asking questions? His tongue was cut out. And last month they killed the chief of the federales for the third time this year. No one wants the job anymore. They took him and raised him on the flagpole—the one with the giant flag, do you know it? The one you can see even from Los Estados? And they ran him to the top.

"How would it look if I let this photographer go without a repercussion? You told me you would always be honest when I hired you, that you would say what you were thinking, even if I did not like it, but you might not understand this, I think. It is not about who killed my son and who did not. It is not about whether I like this photographer. The Zetas will know, after I kill him, that I will come for them next and that perhaps I will run them up the flagpole. If I can kill an American, what can I do to them?

"In the meanwhile, I will make him understand what he needs to see, and the Zetas still won't know about you and the work we are doing together. So please take the men that you can trust—I know you trust at least three of them and have trained them—and make sure he doesn't run and, tomorrow night, allow him to work, and take his camera from him when he is finished."

"Understood," Hull said, and they crossed through the gate into the compound.

7

ELLIS LEANED against the sink as the storm passed over the beach. Lightning illuminated the field outside the kitchen and the ocean beyond the trees. In the following darkness, he felt for the car keys in his pocket. Then he stood looking out at the empty driveway.

"Fuck," he whispered.

He ran the faucet and splashed his face and took an Aguila from the refrigerator and drank it. When he was finished, he opened another beer, his eyes watering from the carbonation. He unlocked the back door and stood inside the entryway, watching the insects that fluttered to the lights under the overhang.

He stepped out onto the patio, listening to the rain on the corrugated roof. His vision flared white, shifted to black, then returned in blues and grays as a peel of thunder followed the lightning.

The pool began to overflow, the water spilling into the brush at the lowest corner of the property. He had seen rain like this, he thought, in Colorado as he was descending the Rockies. Then he had crossed into the desert in Utah.

He had been on the road for five weeks when he met the rancher. He was amazed that day by the sky, open from horizon to horizon along the expanse of the plain.

He stopped for fuel east of Salina and leaned beside the pump, watching the landscape, which was cast in a bronze light that made him think of sepia-toned photos or tintypes. Above the desert a lone thunderhead crawled eastward. The air smelled like pine, and this surprised him— there were few trees—but it was only the scent of the juniper and piñon bushes on the wind.

He reached for his camera and shot a series of landscapes, moving as he worked beyond the gas station. At the top of a hill, he adjusted the f-stop on his aperture to compensate for the low angle of the sun and photographed a crown of light above the thunderhead, followed by the spot of darkness the cloud left as it passed overhead.

When he was finished, he topped off the tank and decided to spend the night in Salina.

The motel was neither clean nor soiled.

He locked his gear into his Pelican case and chained it to the bed frame.

The desert had lost the heat of the day by the time he stepped outside to find dinner.

"The bucket of bones is good," an old man said in the restaurant.

They sat at a bar under the glass eyes of a stuffed antelope. The old man wore cowboy boots. Ellis wore sneakers.

"I've been thinking about trying the buffalo," Ellis said.

"You want buffalo up in Wyoming or the Dakotas," the old man said.

"Here, you should eat the beef. It's good. Mostly local."

"And the bucket's your call?"

"Yes sir. Besides, the ribs are on special."

The old man's hair was pressed in a ring from his hat, which sat beside his elbow on the counter. He smiled when the waitress arrived, and Ellis ordered the ribs and a Pabst Blue Ribbon.

"We're in it together now," the old man said, unfolding his napkin. "I'll have another one, too, please, darling."

When the beers arrived, they sat for a time and drank without speaking. The old man shifted his weight on the stool.

"Where you headed?" the old man asked finally, looking sideways at Ellis.

"I'm not sure yet."

"There's a nice national park just outside of town."

"I drove through it on my way in."

"You're headed west, then. Man, your age should be," he said, and smiled at his own joke. "I'm Jack."

"Robert."

"I didn't mean to force the ribs on you. I'm just particular about my meat. I've been selling cuts to this place for about ten years. Couple other diners and steak houses around the county."

"Is that what you do for work?"

"Ranching."

"And you like it?"

"It's been good, in a way, nice life. I spend my time outside. I like working with the animals. You treat them fair, they'll treat you fair back. I don't like the slaughtering and butchering much, but it's got to be done, and I'd rather do it myself than ship them off and have someone do it wrong."

"Wrong?" Ellis asked, and the old man took another sip from his beer.

"We're about to eat," he said. "You don't want to hear about that particularly."

•

When their food arrived, they ate quietly at the bar, wiping their hands on cloth napkins, which turned red from the sauce. Ellis finished first and watched the rancher clean his plate, picking each rib until no meat remained before laying the bone in a neat pile with the others.

They were drinking another round when Ellis asked if he could take the old man's portrait.

The rancher closed one eye and looked down the neck of his bottle, the lines of his body angular and bony but softened by age and exhaustion.

"I don't know," he said. "It doesn't seem like my thing."

"I have almost no setup for these shoots," Ellis said, and explained the feature for the magazine. "I'll be done in ten minutes. And I don't have to do it tonight. I'm going to be around until tomorrow."

"I'm pretty busy, starting first thing in the morning."

"I'm pretty fast."

"Did you like your ribs?"

"They were probably the best I've ever had."

"Now you're just kissing my ass," the rancher said, and smiled, then grimaced.

He picked up his hat and adjusted it in the mirror and tucked his money under his plate. Ellis stood to shake his hand, but the old man remained seated, looking at himself in the reflection.

"You came in east, right?" the rancher said.

"I'm staying at the La Quinta up the street."

"It's got to be early."

"I have a watch."

"You know where the gas station is off the interstate?"

•

The desert was cold, and the smell of juniper was more pronounced at dawn. Ellis felt a wave of nostalgia for the fall and then winter and then Christmas. He stood watching his breath outside of his room and shivered in his jacket and climbed into the car. He let the engine warm as he checked his equipment. Then he drove to the front of the hotel and found coffee and rolls in the lobby.

He stirred two packets of sugar into a paper cup. The clerk behind the desk said nothing.

When he arrived at the gas station, a pickup truck already sat idling on the far side of the parking lot.

Its headlights flashed once, and he turned to pull in beside it.

The old man cranked open his window. "I don't sleep the way I used to," he said.

"It's cold."

"I've already been to town and dropped some mail in the boxes. We should do this. I've got to get."

"I was actually hoping we could shoot it at your ranch."

The old man looked across the road toward a line of mountains. "I guess," he said into the air, and rolled up his window.

They turned off the paved road after a mile and followed a dirt track that ran north toward a row of foothills. Ellis tried to keep the pickup in sight, but the old man sped across the washboard, stopping occasionally and waiting, then pulling away again, leaving him with only a dust plume to follow.

The ranch came into view two miles out, a trio of low buildings surrounded by fence posts and barbed wire. Then the track dipped, and a cloud of insects snapped across his windshield.

They crossed a corrugated cattle guard onto an expanse of flat land and parked in a courtyard between the buildings. The old man emerged from the main house with a feed pail and scattered shelled corn into the dust for his chickens.

Ellis climbed out of the rental car and locked the doors behind him.

"We can put your cameras in the house if you like," the rancher said. "I know these hens are prone to thievery."

"It's just a habit."

"You sure?"

"Yeah. Sorry. They're already safer than they should have been."

"How's that?" the rancher asked.

"The magazine wanted me to ride a motorcycle for this assignment. Then one of the ad guys couldn't sell the idea to Harley."

"A bike would have been bad in weather."

"It would have been bad in everything."

"Then hallelujah for a lack of salesmanship working in your favor. Let me give you the tour. You can see where you want to shoot this portrait."

They crossed a pasture behind the main house, where two hundred head of cattle grazed. The old man spoke of his livestock stiffly at first, his ease from the night before appearing to have deserted him. Then as the morning wore on, he seemed to almost forget himself and began to speak at length about his herd and fire, drought and sickness, the price of corn, barley, oats, and meal.

He pointed to a diamondback coiled in the shadow of a boulder, and listed the places it would rest in the heat. He described the effects of its venom and spoke of the Hopi, who would dance for the snake to bring rain. Then he described the rain itself, and how the dust smelled when fresh water arrived, and how deeply the earth could crack without moisture.

They ate jerky in the shade of the barn late in the day, sitting next to a rusted calf table. The desert light shone thinly through a window.

Ellis chewed the strips of beef, and as he looked out at the cattle, he saw the clay buildings in Zabul province—men with wooden poles tapping the flanks of goats beside an ancient river.

"Look at this place, dude," a corporal had said to him. "Nothing's changed here since God wrote the Bible."

"How old is ranching?" he asked the old man.

"How old's this ranch?"

"No," he said. "Ranching. The profession?"

"Oh. I don't know. I figure it's old. I guess as soon as man thought up how to build a fence, the first ranch sprung up."

Neither of them mentioned the portrait until they returned to the courtyard, and the day had faded to afterglow.

In New York, Ellis thought, he would not have allowed himself to lose the light, but he felt unrushed and forgiving, even of himself, in the open land.

He looked across the pan at the foothills and the mountains, which grew bluer as the light faded. A sparrow hopped through the underbrush in the chaparral.

Whenever he traveled, he thought, he had come to expect a kind of loneliness, which seemed to add clarity to his photos. He'd also convinced himself that this was necessary, and if he was careful and paid attention to his work, he could carry the things he saw home with him and share them with the people he cared about.

While he stood next to the rancher, it occurred to him that this kind of connection might be impossible, no matter what, even with his images as artifacts.

Then he thought of Kara and his father, and recalled his mother's face, gaunt from cancer. The last time he had seen his father, they hadn't spoken about her in almost two years—they'd barely mentioned her at all since she died when he was eight.

They also hadn't talked about Kara since she left for Morocco. They'd just driven out to the beach to watch the seagulls.

The birds were already eating something at the shoreline but came wheeling overhead when they saw his father carrying bread from the bakery.

"I like her," his father said. "She's been calming you down. She's been good for you. But you're both young. And you both have careers. And you can't expect her to fill in for something we both lost a long time ago."

His father took a piece of bread and threw it out over the snow fence, and Ellis rode the train back into the city and took the assignment to drive to California.

"Shit," the old man said. "I've been chewing your ear all day. A man like you, professional, probably just wants to get the job done."

"We can shoot the portrait tomorrow. I'll come back."

"I hate to make you come out again."

"It's cool. I should probably get to town, or whatever."

"Hell, I got four spare rooms. Stay the night. I'll make dinner."

They washed up at the kitchen sink, which smelled like the rest of the house, of pine and soil. In the courtyard, the old man lit a fire in a cement pit and covered it with a grate. He laid patties of ground beef over the coals and roasted two ears of corn in their husks. He poked the fire with a brand as they stood and warmed their hands over the flames. Then he toasted two buns and butterflied chilies and blackened them on the grate.

They sat in folding chairs beside the pit and ate, the juices from the beef dripping down their forearms. When they were finished, Ellis zipped his coat, and the old man buttoned his own lean frame into a denim jacket, turning the wool-lined collar up on his neck.

Their eyes dried, then began to water as the wind shifted and caught the smoke.

The coals pulsed with the breeze, the embers tinkling when they shifted, a sound without weight.

"I like this place," Ellis said. "I forget sometimes why I shoot photos to begin with."

The old man had tucked his chin into his collar, but now he raised it to look at the photographer.

"How's that?" he asked.

"I don't know," Ellis said.

"Well, why do it?"

"I like what I see when I look at people. It makes me notice things. I guess I like the places it takes me. Or some of them."

"And you like this?"

"Yeah. It's beautiful."

"I agree."

"And quiet."

"Sometimes."

"Am I talking too much?"

"No. I'm just pulling your leg. You listened to me all day going on about ranching."

"It's just that I work with people who've forgotten why they started shooting," he said, and found a lens cap in his pocket and picked at it with his nails and looked away from the old man and back to the fire. "And they don't even realize it's happened. And I can feel that happening to me. When I was in school, I remember I'd go to class or the darkroom, or whatever, and we'd talk about how one little change in the emulsion could affect everything. And I couldn't put down the camera. And even when I did, I was thinking about photos. It kept me awake sometimes. It kept me awake a lot, actually. I'd just get up and walk around the city at night shooting. Now that just seems exhausting."

"Lots of people's work is," the old man said.

"I know."

"Do you?"

"No. I mean, yeah. I know."

"I was at the slaughterhouse for thirty-seven years."

"What made you walk away and open this place?"

"I had the money to. That's part."

"What else?"

"You ever been to a slaughterhouse?"

In the distance Ellis could hear the cattle in the field, the grinding of their hooves, the inhalation of their breath. The fire popped, sparks rising above the grate.

"We used to bring them in," the old man said. "All types of cattle. And we'd take them and process them, and for a long time for me, that was that—there just wasn't a whole lot to it. We drove them into the box, and we'd use stun bolts on them and then bleed them on the rail, send them on down the line for quartering. It was about as humane as it gets.

"Some countries, Third World mostly, cut the spinal cord. It's tricky work, and the cow knows it's being cut and bled. Or they use hammers or electricity. The cattle spasm so hard, it breaks their backs. The Kiwis, they actually have a pretty good electric stun, sophisticated, cow can't feel pain.

"Anyway, they'd score us on how efficient we were with the bolt. And they'd call it a stun, but it's really a kill. Anything below ninety-five percent accuracy, you'd get bounced off the gun. Management wanted one shot, first shot, almost every time, cow needs to go down, senseless. Right through the brain, up on the forehead."

He demonstrated with his fingers.

"It's a little different on goats and pigs. So I'm good with the gun, but after a while I realize, well, like everyone else, I get an eye for the cattle. Which ones are sick, which ones are pregnant. You can see it in their gait sometimes, the way they hold their head—their eyes, too, if they're watering.

"Now the pregnant ones, they'll have a soft spot if you touch them near the base of the tail, and you're supposed to cut them out of the herd before they're even loaded. And if they are loaded, before they're unloaded at the house. And then if they're unloaded at the house, before they're drove up to the stun box. They don't make it up to the box much. Ranchers themselves usually inseminate the cattle, so to them, to us, that's just money growing inside. We've put it in there. Why send it to the houses?

"But you can't control everything, especially on a ranch, and outfits that move a lot of head—and you know how it is—they slip through, even to the box sometimes, and there's no real legalities to protect them. Some guys would stun them, and that would be that. I got a few, too, by mistake when I was younger.

"Anyway, one day, I see a guy down the line, he'd probably been there thirty-five years. Jim Harlan was his name. He goes to make the slaughter cut, and he sees that this cow is pregnant. I mean, *real* pregnant.

"She's been hit with the stun by another guy already, so there's nothing Jim can do really, but he whets his knife, which was already razor-fucking-sharp, and he goes and he cuts open her belly. And holy shit, out comes this calf, right there on the killing room floor, and it's thrashing around before the membrane's even off its head, slipping in the blood.

"So he wrestles it still, which is easy, and gets the caul off, and now there're supervisors there watching this, and one of them wants the guy with the gun to hit the calf too—she's sort of upsetting the other animals.

"Well Jim says no fucking way—he just delivered this thing, you know, so he takes the calf and hoses it down real gentle and plops it in the bed of his pickup. Then he doesn't come back for the rest of the day. I guess he drove the thing out to his house. Someone told me he still has it, but that was a long time ago.

"Anyway, he shows up for work the next morning, and they pink-slip him for stealing company property and walking off the jobsite. Just like that. I guess they figured that calf was theirs, bought and paid for, same as those hours Jim took in the middle of the day shift.

"I did the same thing as Jim for a few years after that. Most would be stillborn, but shit, I got about six live ones. They say—someone told me once—that about ten percent of all the cattle that's slaughtered are pregnant. That sounds high to me, but it was hard to tell. You'd feel the calves kicking sometimes, inside, and it was real obvious in those instances. And shit, I just couldn't disappear with them in the middle of the day. I needed the income. I had a cap on the bed of my truck then. Most times, I'd just put them in there, and they'd lie down, and I'd pull around somewhere and park it in the shade. They can't walk for a few hours anyway.

"I told myself it offset all the death, that saving a few was right. I'm not so sure anymore, but it made me feel better long enough to keep working and to keep saving my money. I helped them survive, and they helped me get up every day so I could come here and have this.

"I still slaughter them. I have to. But I give them a life first, and they grow up here, and they're well fed and cared for, and it's that part now, the living, not just the death, that's the thing I know how to do. It wasn't easy, though. Seems like it shouldn't have been, I guess."

●

Ellis photographed the old man the next morning in natural light before the sun grew too harsh. He set a high ISO speed on his Canon to give the photos grain and focused on the catchlight in the old man's irises. He shifted the RAW files to monochrome and checked them on the digital monitor and then loaded a roll of black-and-white film into his Hasselblad.

The rancher was smiling a little in the best portrait, his teeth hidden behind as he looked straight into the camera. The lines of his face were suited to the contrasts of the medium-format film—the white stubble anchored in his oversized pores, the dark crease across the bridge of his nose where it had broken and healed.

They shook hands when Ellis was finished, and the old man helped him load his gear into the rental car. In New York, the editors passed over the old man's portrait. They had run a photo of a boy in a Stetson instead, who was leaning beside a cow pen, typing a text message.

8

HULL LAY in the bedroom of the guesthouse, unsure of what had woken him—maybe something within himself, maybe something without. Motionless, he listened to the metallic drum of the rain on the tin roof and the flat spatter on the palms leaves outside. The runoff seemed to gurgle into the corner of his garden, a deeper sound from the gutters, sluicing into the mud.

He reached out and slid his hand behind the bedside table and felt for the wooden grip of his shotgun. Then he lay still again. Projecting ahead, he anticipated the motions of his body and the duct tape tearing from the backside of the dresser, the weight of the gun drawing the bolt closed to feed the shell into the chamber.

He looked over at the angle of the wall and the defilade it created from the doorway. He heard the dry flutter of cockroach wings against the tile floor. The insect went silent, then landed with a soft click, fluttered, and lifted off again down the hallway.

He drew his hand back under the sheets. He closed his eyes, still listening, and felt his position on the mattress, the throbbing in his knees as he adjusted his legs.

The rivulets on the windowpane made small shifts in the darkness on the far wall. He rolled over and placed a pillow between his thighs and let the weight from his hip rest against the cushion. He sat up and rubbed his knees.

He had been on a foot patrol in La Libertad when the rebels sent an

RPG into a restaurant on the waterfront, the rocket hissing past the pillars along the patio, missing them all somehow, before it arced harmlessly out to sea.

At first, he assumed the line of fire had originated from the hillside above the beach, and he turned to check the jungle. Then a salvo of light arms came from his left, and he saw that the ambush had been set in a cemetery ahead of them.

He could smell pupusas cooking in the kitchen as he knelt to return fire, and a cloud of bats scattered from a tree above the tombstones. He had been with the Special Operations Group for six months, attached through Fort Bragg to the Special Activities Division and through the SAD to the Salvadoran Army.

He had seen enough by then to know that the squad would not fall back to a new position. Instead, they would run directly into the restaurant and through the crowd on the patio.

He screamed and ordered them to turn north as the bats swooped in low over their heads along with the zip of passing gunfire. He wanted the men to displace into an alley so he could decide whether to egress or reengage from cover. Then a sergeant named Claros, who liked to smoke Partagas, and who had a wife in the capital and an apartment off Calle El Mirador with a crucifix above their door, was hit in the neck, and the guerillas began firing with a mounted machine gun.

The cyclic rate had suggested the weapon was a Russian PKM 7.62 mm. Hull didn't remember the concussion from the next RPG, but he did remember crawling in the street after the blast, dragging his smoking legs behind a collapsed column of concrete, then leaning against the remains of a man wearing an apron.

He remembered the call button on his bedside table at Walter Reed, the haze of medication, and the water burning in his legs each time they came with the irrigator.

Now he checked his watch and stood stiffly and crossed the room.

In the closet, he took down his jungle pants and leaned against the wall to step into them. He pulled on his boots and tied the laces and cinched the ankle cuffs on each leg. He buttoned his shirt and slipped his phone into the chest pocket. There was a precision to his movements in the dark, a rote procedure as he dressed.

He took a flashlight from the top shelf and clicked it on and off to check the batteries. Then he buckled the straps of a leg holster and slid the flashlight into his waistband and pulled a long, plastic poncho from the rack and drew it over his head.

At a clay pot in the corner, he reached past a plastic liner to retrieve his pistol. Bringing the Sig Sauer close to his chest, he inched the slide back and checked the chamber.

Downstairs, he pulled the skirt up on the poncho and secured the gun in his leg holster. The rain seemed louder than it had been in the bedroom. He checked his access to the weapon, smoothed the anorak back into place, and unlocked the door.

He stepped over a series of puddles and peered around the corner of the guesthouse at his garden. His eyes followed a drainage pipe, which ran from the roof, where the rainwater was being channeled directly into the flower bed.

He shook his head and returned to the front of the house.

In the driveway, he unlocked the door to a Jeep Cherokee with plates from Virginia. He turned the engine over and drove downhill toward the gate.

Across the compound, lights still burned in the hacienda's windows, and he imagined the jefe awake somewhere inside, eating, watching television, walking the hallways. He switched on the Cherokee's headlights, and the raindrops seemed to form a sheet beyond the windshield, almost silver in the glare, which forced him to lean forward in order to read the road.

The guards stared through the rain as he drove past the gate, turning in their ponchos, their own weapons also dry beneath the plastic. He steered the truck around the rut flooded with rainfall and descended the hill toward the ocean.

At the fork, he turned west and switched off the lights, following the track that led to the beach house. He braked and waited for his eyes to adjust and drove the rest of the way in the dark.

It was difficult for him to find the Prado at first because his men had parked it under a stand of palms. Beyond the fronds, he could see a single light inside of the kitchen.

He sat for a while, shifting his attention back and forth from the house to the truck. Something about the position of the Cherokee under the trees, with its dead, unlit gauges on the dashboard, reminded him again of El Salvador—the mountains near the Río Torola where he had found the cockpit of an embassy helicopter smoldering in the forest.

The memory was so liminal and fleeting that he wondered if he'd had it at all, even as he pushed it away.

He'd spent so much time searching for why suddenly his mind would return to the war—revisiting the faces of the men he had known, or the bodies of the children on the roadside, long after they were gone. Sometimes there was a trigger or a pattern he could follow. The way a road lay on a hill near his house or the ditch running beside it would overlap with the position of a machine gun post he had overrun in Usulután. The sound of a screw falling from his fingers, bouncing across the concrete in his garage, would become the broken plates under his legs in the ruined restaurant.

Other times, there seemed to be no triggers at all—the memories were simply there, unfolding against the present, a door opening between this instant and some other place and decade. Perhaps it was that he recognized patterns he should be able to read but could not yet. More often he found that the connections he made in a field, or in his room when he woke up, which seemed so much like something from his past, were only creations of his mind.

He also found that his memories had the potential to evolve each time he revisited them, so that now the Jeep in the rain under the trees would be associated with the helicopter. And the gauges on the Jeep would be with him in the dark at the crash site in the highlands.

It was as if the Cherokee had actually been there, even though he could sit and tell himself that this was only some flaw in his memory, a disjointed trick of time.

He looked away from the dashboard and reached for his cell phone. The Prado's driver picked up after the second ring.

"I'm behind you," Hull said. "I'm coming up."

He stepped out of the truck, watching the driveway and the windows for any movement. He crossed the space between the vehicles and slid into the back seat of the Prado, smoothing the poncho around him.

The inside of the cab smelled like coffee and sweat, and maybe rum. A nightscope rested on the dashboard.

"*Una grande tormenta,*" he said to the two men, the Spanish on his tongue lagging just behind the Spanish in his thoughts, a gap he had been unable to close since the language section of the Q Course.

"*Sí,*" said the driver.

"*El fotógrafo?*"

"He's no sleeping yet."

"No?"

The man in the passenger's seat took the scope and handed it to Hull. "*Él está en el patio,*" he said.

"*En la lluvia?*"

"*Bajo el toldo.*"

Hull followed the lines of the house to the overhang and found Ellis through the rain and the undergrowth.

Magnified in green tones, the photographer stood watching the rain-fall with an open beer beside him. His face was smooth, and his body was thin with the lines of a runner.

Hull had already been in the Special Forces for five years by the time he was the photographer's age. His father had been to Korea and come back as an officer. His uncle had gone to Vietnam at twenty and come home after his second tour, wrapped in the flag.

He had seen much younger men killed, and killed them himself during his time with the SAD. Claros had only been twenty-six the day on the waterfront.

It was spring in Virginia.

He could always plant another garden, he told himself, as long as it was somewhere cool and where he could sit in the new house with his legs by the fire in winter. Then he wouldn't need to read in Spanish at the grocery store, and the power would only die in bad weather.

"How long has he been sitting there?" he asked.

"*No sé,*" said the man in the passenger's seat.

"*Una hora,*" answered the driver. "*Más o menos. Más posiblemente.*"

•

Ellis climbed the stairs to the bedroom sometime after two in the morning.

He fell asleep quickly, but first he saw São Paulo, where helicopters ferried the rich from skyscraper to skyscraper, high above the favelas. Drifting with the sound of the rain, he watched a teenager walk toward him on thin legs in ragged pants. As they passed one another, he reached into his pocket to check for his wallet and thought of how many meals the boy could buy with his camera equipment.

The pillowcases under his head smelled of detergent—cornflower-blue bottle, the brand Kara used when they did laundry. Behind his eyes, he watched as they sat together in a restaurant in the Bowery, toward the end of their relationship, each home from foreign assignments. New York had been changed for them in the time they'd spent away from it—the trains louder, the drinks colder, the buildings taller and sharper.

Almost everything was different in those first few days as they adjusted to being home, and readjusted to each other. Their own faces were unfamiliar in some ways, as if the details they had remembered in each other were gone, replaced by new ones.

"You look different," she said.

It was quiet and very dark in her apartment. The heat from the radiator made her skin dry and smooth, and the moonlight through the window cast a line across her body.

He drifted down into the scent of soap, toward the points of her hip bones.

In the morning, she told him about the assignment in Morocco.

"I want it to rain all day today," she said.

"When are you leaving?"

"Next week."

"We should stay in bed if it does. I think it's going to stop though."

"I still have jet lag," she said.

"Me too."

"Can you sleep more?"

"I can always sleep."

"Let's sleep, then," she said, and he looked across at the photos of her family taped to the walls, which seemed to be filled to the edges with her sisters and her parents, along with her aunts and her cousins.

She had a different haircut, he saw, in each image, but her body seemed to lean into the frame in the same way, like she'd just run over from the camera.

In one photo, he noticed three black lines tattooed across the inside of one wrist, which was how he had always known her. In most of the others, he saw, they were missing.

It was warm in the bed, and she was touching his ankle with her foot.

"Are you still awake?" she whispered.

"I think my jet lag is working against me."

"Close your eyes."

"I'm trying."

"We're probably not going to sleep."

"I want to."

"Then what is it?"

"I'm just thinking."

"About Morocco?"

"About us always leaving."

"I know," she said.

"I thought we were going to be in the city for a while."

"I'm sorry."

"It's cool. I'm just tired."

"We're too young to be tired."

"I'm still tired anyway," he said.

She rolled over and swept her bangs out of her eyes. "Are you getting old on me?"

"Maybe."

"You father says you were born nomadic."

"That's just something he tells himself."

"He loves you. You guys look like each other."

"Sometimes I wish there was more for him to think about. It was always just the two of us."

"Not always," she said.

"Yeah."

"I told you he showed me her picture that time we visited."

"He's the one getting old, then."

"She was pretty."

"I don't really remember. Where are they sending you?"

"Casablanca. Then the Western Sahara. Then we'll be based in Marrakesh. They have some condo for me and the writer and the other photographer. And they're going to send over an editor and an art director a couple times. And maybe a videographer."

"That's a lot of moving parts."

"It's a cover package for their North Africa issue, or whatever."

"You going to the Atlases?"

"Probably."

"I've never been to North Africa."

"I heard the weather's like Southern California."

"I heard the goats climb trees."

"I heard the light's insane."

"We should check out some Capa."

"I'm going to get some Bowles and Burroughs."

"I haven't read Bowles."

"Me either."

"I've read Burroughs. Don't read *Naked Lunch.*"

"That shit's crazy," she said. "I read it at RISD."

"My mag wants me on the road next month," he said. "Something like a cross between Richard Avedon and William Eggleston. They're going to get me a motorcycle or something and a deal with Motel 6."

"That sounds cool," she said, and laughed.

"It could be."

"It sounds like they're pushing you."

"They just want as much as they can get for their retainer."

"They want it to be good though."

"Of course they want it to be good. They'll also use it all up if you let them."

"So don't let them," she said.

"I'm trying not to."

"You're always saying that. I don't know if you are, really."

He moved his foot away from hers. "You're going to be gone for a while."

"I wanted to talk about that."

"Let's get up," he had said. "We still have a couple of days, or whatever."

9

HULL CROSSED into the compound just before daybreak and parked the Jeep and unlocked his office in the blockhouse. At his desk, he picked up the receiver on an encrypted landline and dialed his man at the border.

"*Esta noche,*" he said to the Nicaraguan, who clicked his tongue, sounding tired.

"*Estuve allí anoche,*" the guard said.

"*Comprendo,*" Hull said. "*Pero esta noche te pagaremos doble.*"

"*Doble?*"

"*Sí. Pero tú*—you have to stamp his papers. The photographer's passport. It has to have a Nicaraguan seal. Nicoyan federal police, the OIF. They need to think he crossed into your country. *Si no estampes su pasaporte, no te pagamos. Entiendes?*"

"*Bueno. Yo lo estampo. Estaré alla. Esta noche. El puesto siete.*"

"*De acuerdo,*" Hull said, and dialed his two computer techs, the Texans in their early twenties who were originally white hats when he found them working in tiger teams in San Quintín.

"*Buenos días,*" the one from Dallas said with his slower drawl.

"Keep me on speaker," Hull said. "Can you both hear me?"

"We can hear you. Where do you want to start?"

"We always start at the macro level."

"You're the boss," the one from Houston said. "We broke into a few emails from that faction of Zetas up in TJ about an hour ago. Just traffic, back and forth. Nothing we can use, really. They're smarter than most of the other operations. I dropped the text translations into your box on the server about five minutes ago."

"Any other intercepts?"

"It seems like, based on the volume of chatter between Tijuana and León, a shipment might be coming up the Gulf Coast from Columbia. The package may be set for transfer north at the end of the month. We're having trouble breaking full encryption, though, so we have a handful of emails and texts without a complete snapshot of the context. They're communicating in volume, though, and one exchange had some suggestive long and lat coordinates, so you'll have to check out the packet. That's also in the box on the server."

"What about the photographer?" Hull asked, and the Texans both sighed into the speaker.

"That situation is the same as yesterday," the one from Houston said. "We think his phone's still off. Well, it is still off, to be exact, not that it matters with the signal inhibitor. Plus there's no internet down there at the beach house. And no outgoing on the landline, either."

"He's in a box," the one from Dallas said.

"Keep me updated."

"*No problemo.*"

After he hung up, he opened his computer and scanned the text uploads in his inbox. It was still early, he realized. He counted the hours until Padaratz was scheduled to land at the airport. Then he dialed each member of the three-man surveillance detail assigned to monitor the photographer and explained one final time what would be expected of them at the fights.

He dangled the headset in his fingers when he was finished, tired of speaking Spanish. The sun had begun to burn through the clouds, a flare of heat on his skin.

He pressed the receiver to clear the line and called his men in the Prado. "He still sleeping," the driver said.

In the garden, Hull dug a ditch away from the depression where the runoff had emptied into the mud. The earth was soft and he worked quickly. He angled the drainage downhill into the grass and found a length of PVC in the gardener's shed on the far side of the compound. Working back along the ditch with the shovel, he set the plastic tubing into the earth and joined the pipe to the gutter mouth with a downspout.

The loose soil of the ditch was dark against the bright lawn.

He checked his watch and knelt to pick at his plants, moving to the dogwood tree, touching the sapling lightly with his fingers.

•

Ellis rolled over in the bed and pulled on his sneakers. His clothes still carried the smell of the pits, a mixture of lard and copper. In the kitchen, he made coffee as he looked out at the empty driveway. He set his cup on the counter without taking a sip and brought his bags down from the closet. He loaded his lenses and camera into his backpack and tried to recall where along the road from Iberia he had passed a bus station.

He unplugged the coffee pot and counted his cash—six hundred and fifty American, maybe eighty more in colónes. He tucked the local currency into his sock and locked the rest of the money in the safe beside his passport.

His watch was still set for the time in New York, and he wound the

Rolex back two hours. The sky was dark with clouds, making it feel much earlier.

He walked to the window and splashed his face at the sink and revisited the conversation with the jefe and what he'd said about putting him on another flight and how, at six, they were supposed to send a car to take him back to the arena. He listened for a dial tone on the house line and turned on his cell phone, pacing while it searched for a signal. Then he switched it off.

Two of the walls in the living room were wired with phone jacks, but neither included a hardline to the internet. The tile was cold under his knee as he knelt beside the second outlet, which was filled with some kind of melted plastic.

Outside, the pool filter clicked on, and he moved to the window to look at the water. A truck was parked in the track past the back gate, under a cluster of palm trees.

He paced around the kitchen again toward the safe, only to turn back to the counter, and sat down and pulled the car keys from his pocket and found the jerky. He opened the door to the patio and drifted away from the house, into the field, its dead grass flattened and waterlogged. He ducked under the wasps' nest and began to run when he reached the black sand at the edge of the property.

•

"*Está corriendo*," the Prado's driver said through the earpiece. "*En la playa*."

Hull cradled the cell phone between his jaw and shoulder and watched a spider mite crawl into a bract on the dogwood tree.

"Is he running or jogging?" he asked.

"*No se.*"

"Is he exercising?"

"He also pack his bags, señor."

"He didn't bring them, correct?"

"*Sus bolsas?* He no take them with him."

"He's on the beach?"

"Yes."

"Not on the road?"

"He is no on the road."

"Alright," Hull said, and translated each item he wanted from the beach house, repeating the safe's master code slowly in Spanish. "*Pasaporte,*" he said. "*Dinero. Claro?*"

10

AT THE river mouth, the beach had been smoothed and reshaped overnight by the rain. Ellis scanned along the sand, searching for the puppies' footprints. When he reached the nest, he knelt and touched the turtle eggs—an organic plastic. At the foot of the berm, he followed a section of beach where the dogs' tracks had been erased by the tide, then found them again running along the riverbank, overwritten by the footprints of birds and lizards.

He squatted under a palm tree, which was growing almost parallel to the slope, and pulled the jerky from his pocket. The clouds broke up over the ocean, and vultures circled in a gyre, riding the first thermal of the day in the growing light.

Sweating into his shirt, he whistled and held his breath near the edge of the jungle, listening to the buzz of cicadas rising around him.

He was about to turn back for the house when one of the puppies came into view within the undergrowth. She was so thin that she looked more like an apparition to him than something living. She had survived for about six weeks, he guessed—bone and hide moving across the sand.

She pressed her ears flat and skulked through the beach grass with her head and back bowed, her shoulder blades moving slowly. When she reached the edge of the jungle and would come no farther, she sat and whined softly, watching him, coiled and suspicious.

He tore away a shred of jerky and tossed it at her feet—and she followed the meat with her off-color eyes, but remained sitting, shifting her attention between the food in his hand and the scrap in the grass beside her. The edges of her nostrils spread, her wide head tracing small circles in the air as she ran her tongue out to lick her jowls.

He began to tear another piece of jerky, and she pulled away very quickly now, toward the jungle. He waited until she finally became settled again before he tossed a second scrap of jerky beside the first piece—and the puppy flinched but did not run, looking from him to the food and back toward the undergrowth.

In the heat, she moved so slowly toward the meat that he almost lost sight of her in the thick grass within the palm's shadow. Then the wind blew in from the west and cooled the sweat on his back, smelling of the ocean, along with a hint of something dead at the river.

When she ate, she hunched over the scraps and lay down in the sand and looked up at him expectantly. He watched her one blue eye, and she cocked her head, appraising him. He held the last piece of meat out, flat in his palm, his legs aching from crouching.

This time, she stood almost immediately and pulled the meat from his hand, flinching again when he touched her, cowering at his feet.

He waited for her to finish, then scooped her from the sand and cradled her against his chest, whispered to her softly. In the underbrush closer to the river, he found her twin, its chest motionless, a fly flickering across its iris. He turned away and started back for the beach house, the living puppy warm against his ribs, licking his arm as he walked.

•

On the porch the puppy studied him with her blue eye through the doorway, panting under the overhang, her stomach pressed into a puddle. He took a cardboard box out of the pantry and emptied it and lined it with a sheet from the bedroom.

"You can come inside," he said, and she cocked her ear. "You need a place to sleep."

When something moved in the hair on his arm, he reached down and felt an alien smoothness—a tick in the crease of his elbow, which he pinched and flicked into the bushes. Then he ran his hands through his hair and along the folds of his ears and found another tick clinging to his T-shirt.

He put the dog in the box and carried them both upstairs into the bathroom and stripped and showered quickly, checking his crotch and armpits. He placed the puppy into the tub at his feet, where she appeared even thinner and younger, shivering under the faucet. A flea wriggled up from her coat as he shampooed her back. Other dark flecks also appeared in the foam, along with another tick, swollen with blood, its abdomen the size of an acorn, writhing its legs, carried by the muddy current toward the drain. He combed her fur with his fingers and found more fleas, which disappeared into the soap when he tried to pinch them.

In the bedroom, he dried her with a towel and fed her a piece of a granola bar from his backpack. She shivered and drank lamely from a bowl of water he had filled from the tap. Then she lay down in the box, still shivering in the cool air.

She rose almost immediately and lowered her backside over the tiles. A puddle expanded across the floor beneath her haunches, thin and nearly clear, which caused him to place her back into the shower.

Frightened now, she jumped out of the stall and stood between his feet, so he sat down and pulled her against him and ran her hind legs under the faucet. Once she was clean, he turned off the water, and she pressed her head into his palm and closed her eyes, and he watched her dream, her jaw working, her legs twitching and eyelids fluttering.

She woke in what seemed to be a passing moment of terror, and he saw the blue iris. Then she shifted her head in his hand and blinked, a sweep of long, black eyelashes.

A flea leapt from her back onto his arm, and he caught it and broke it open at the abdomen with his thumbnail. Flicking it away, he set her head down and pushed himself up from the floor. She continued to sleep as he cleaned the tiles, mopping the puddle with the same towel he had used to dry her body.

She seemed to be dreaming again when he left her and went down into the kitchen. He dropped the towel into the trash at the island and opened his computer and looked at the photos of the puppies from the previous morning. They appeared nearer to the lens now than he remembered, and he could tell them apart from the widths of their skulls and their brindles.

It had been a long time since his camera had offered any distance from his subjects. The puppy looked different to him than she would have a year ago, he decided. Even his own life had seemed removed once through the glass.

Now he saw a series of possible futures—his father's backyard with its bird feeder, the light box at the magazine, Kara's pale shoulder, a small house somewhere green and quiet. For some reason it had always been easier for him to imagine how it might feel if his photos could buy him whatever his friends possessed rather than what he really wanted.

It dawned on him that he never actually knew what he wanted, other than to keep shooting, and to keep traveling, and to have his photos published. Maybe something had changed in Afghanistan, he thought.

It might have begun when Kara left for Morocco.

Maybe it was changing now, too late.

•

He slept through the afternoon and woke with insect bites on his ankles. When the dog heard him moving on the mattress, she slunk from her box and shat in the bathroom.

He cleaned her haunches again, then wiped the floor and refilled her water.

She went back to her box without drinking, and he ran his finger along her nose, which was dry like leather. He set a piece of a granola bar near the water bowl and touched her ear.

"This makes zero sense," he whispered.

A Toyota Prado approached and parked across from the house, replacing the one under the palm trees.

The driver honked, and he closed the bedroom door behind him and picked up his backpack and walked out to the truck, the bag heavy with his cameras.

North

Hull

•

HE SITS close to the window with frost in its panes, filled with flat November sky. The room is warm from the oven, and his father sits at the head of the table. Outside, the crows peck at the suet his father hung earlier.

He watches them eat—his father, his grandfather, his uncle. His father works around his plate, separating the meat from the bones with his fingers. He wipes his hands carefully on the napkin in his lap and takes up his fork, then pushes the potatoes and the cranberries onto the tines. He pins the dark meat on last, and each bite he assembles is almost identical.

His father does not look up from his plate—he has cooked all day, standing over the wood grill in the cold to smoke the turkey. His hair is not gray yet, but something about his face, with its hawk nose and eyes that turn down at the corners, makes him look much older than even the principal at Hull's high school.

His grandfather, who eats quickly and erratically like a child, begins to tell a joke from the foot of the table. His uncle leans forward to listen, and his mother turns to whisper with his grandmother. His uncle's girlfriend, who is new again this year, inserts herself into their conversation. His grandfather does impressions with a slab of breast meat in his mouth—the voices of a drunk and a cop beside an empty interstate.

The drunk in this one has been pulled over for weaving back and forth across the median. They're both out of their cars, on the shoulder in the dark, beside a cattle ranch, where a black steer is pacing back and forth on the far side of the fence, snorting occasionally, watching them from under his horns.

The drunk is slurring his words and slouching.

"You been tipping it?" his grandfather asks as the cop, and switches voices and answers.

"Not a drop, Officer," he says.

"Like hell."

"I'm sober as a priest. Look at me. I'm sober as the judge who'll dismiss this case."

"I saw you pull out of Lance's Tavern three miles back. You've been doing zigzags since, all the way up the interstate."

"There was a hornet in the cab," the drunk answers. "He just flew out the window right this minute, I swear it. You want me to stand on one leg? How about I walk that white line? See that fence? How about I walk that rail? I'll walk as straight as the part in your hair. I won't even need pomade."

"How about I lock you in the drunk tank?"

"Now wait a minute now."

"You smell like you took a bath with Johnnie and rinsed your mouth out with Jose."

"You get people out here walking lines and perching like cranes. You send them on their way?"

"Let's start with you standing up straight."

"My posture's bad, that's all, it's the scoliosis."

"Bourbon curves the spine," the cop says. "I've heard that. I think I read it in the *Annals of Medical Bullshit*. Or maybe it was the *Field Manual for Highway Patrolmen*."

"I'm not much of a reader myself," the drunk says. "Either way, if I walk that fence there, right on top of the high rail, one post to another, it doesn't matter. Seems like if I walk that fence, I'm sober enough to operate this pickup. It only does fifty-five, and I only live five miles, maybe six more up the interstate."

"How about you walk the line. Then maybe I let you stand on one leg."

"I make it through them, I walk that fence?"

"You don't shut up right now, I call this in and take your keys away."

"Alright," the drunk says, "let me see here, let me stand on one leg."

He pulls himself upright and stands motionless, smirking at the officer. Then he wobbles off down the line of the breakdown lane.

On the other side of the fence, the longhorn follows him up and back again, blowing air and pawing at the dust in the paddock. The drunk mumbles something to the animal, but the cop can't make it out, because a semi roars past out in the roadway.

"How'd you like how I stood on one leg?"

"You did the tests out of order."

"How'd you like how I walked that lane?"

"Almost nice and straight."

"How about I walk that fence there, then, like we discussed, and we'll see what happens?"

Without waiting for an answer, the drunk climbs up and balances on the top of the split rail and walks from one post to another.

The bull follows again, blowing and huffing, and the drunk says something else to the animal.

They're both nearly back to the police cruiser when the drunk whips off his belt, sails down from the rail, and wrestles the longhorn to the ground and hog-ties it.

"Jesus H.," the cop says as the drunk stumbles over the fencing.

"You like how I stood on one leg?"

"Yeah. I figure."

"You like how I walked that lane?"

"I guess. Absolutely."

"You like how I walked that rail, one post to the other?"

"I have to say."

"Good," the drunk says, and Hull's grandfather takes a sip of his Black

Label. "And how about what I did to that big nigger on the bicycle? Son of a bitch kept trying to distract me."

Hull can see the specks of turkey on his grandfather's tongue as he laughs. He can see the scar on his uncle's face, which is also new this year, where the nerve was severed, and the place where his cheek droops a little as he smiles. He can hear his father's fork working around his plate beside him.

He looks at his uncle's girlfriend for as long as he can without her noticing and watches the way she makes brief eye contact with his mother, a blinked recognition, a sense of embarrassment and apology that he doesn't quite understand yet but intuits that it is reserved for everyone else in the family.

It has begun to snow outside the window, and the crows are still flapping around the suet in the dusting. Hull has heard this joke before and others like it. He's fourteen and is the youngest person at the table.

When his father shot and killed a man near the Chosin Reservoir in Korea, he was only twenty. He was with a squad in a ditch with a stream running along its length that had frozen over. His father was nearly close enough to touch the Chinese scout, who had already thrown a grenade and was raising his rifle.

Hull has never spoken about this with his father. It's his uncle, who is close enough in age to be Hull's brother, who's always told him the stories no one else will about their family.

Once, Hull did find a photo in their attic of his father standing near a dead body. The print was hidden in the type of desk that men convert to workbenches. It was with his father's paystubs and the hammer he kept in the house for hanging pictures and the oil he used to lubricate the door hinges. It was in a file with a seal on the cover from the US Army. It lay beneath other paperwork in the type of drawer that other fathers would use to hide a pinup mag or a bottle.

His father was much thinner then, and his legs looked incredibly long because of the way they seemed to cut fatigues in the 1950s. The pool under the Chinese soldier was black in the monochrome image, and the bead of the surface tension made the blood look like melted wax on the frozen stream bank.

The other officers around his father were standing apart, careful of the pool and their footsteps. His father was stooping a little, bowed in his back, staring indirectly at the body. His face seemed blank, like he was trying to draw himself in from some foreign place, out of thought, and back to reality.

His uncle told him something that his father had relayed once—that the last thing his father remembered, before aligning his sight picture on the scout, was watching thousands of shards of ice, which flew shining from the stream in the ditch, thrown up by the explosion behind him.

Now his father feeds their dog a piece of turkey under the table. Watching him, Hull thinks about how, this morning in the kitchen, his father scooped a spider into a jar with a scrap of mail, then released it, riding a line of silk down from the window.

The room smells like the onions his father browned in a pan earlier, and there are small bits of flour on his father's sleeve, which he stirred in to thicken the gravy. His mother and grandmother are still discussing the book they've been reading, and his uncle's new girlfriend is now moving a little more easily through their conversation.

She's twenty-one, like his uncle, and is in her junior year at the University of California in San Diego. She's never been to Virginia before. She hasn't read this particular novel but rather another one from the same author. It sounds like, in her opinion, as if the writer is still sifting through similar themes and characters.

His grandfather and uncle are both focused on their plates, eating again silently. They share the same eye color, a pale milky blue that Hull sees when he looks in the mirror. It reminds him of a river they drove beside once on a family vacation in Newfoundland, the water carrying ice melt and sandy volcanic silica. He imagines his grandfather hunched over his bombsight in the nose cone of a Liberator, the inboard engine on the port wing disabled, the glass smudged with soot from flak bursts ranged to their altitude of formation.

According to his uncle, his grandfather flew fifty-one missions without a Purple Heart, though he crash-landed twice, and a shorn roof panel left his first pilot decapitated. Most of this information is relayed in statistics—tasked three times to bomb the oil fields in Ploešti, skimming across the Med one hundred feet from the deck out of an airstrip in Libya. On their second run to the refinery, they lost 660 men over Romania. The Germans had cracked their radio code and were waiting for them with 10.5-centimeter 38s, 88-millimeter canons, and Messerschmitts.

The only outward evidence he's seen of his grandfather's time in Europe is the Ninth Air Force ring he sometimes wears on his finger. The signet always makes Hull think of his grandfather's hand hovering over the bomb switch, and the people on the ground he killed from a vertical distance. The scar on his uncle's face provokes something similar—his arm jerking a lanyard to fire artillery into the Song Ngan Valley—even though it came from a car accident near Camp Pendleton after his first tour in country.

He wonders what other people see when they see them together—the tic his father has of scanning back over his shoulders in public, the pale wolf eyes of his uncle and grandfather, the way they tell certain jokes too loudly.

He wonders what his uncle's new girlfriend could possibly think of his family. He has the same eye color as his uncle and grandfather, the same nose as his father. He's the only male at the table who has not killed another human.

For a moment he sees them and himself in the new way that she does—and in the old understanding of his mother, a prism of violent and confusing contradictions.

His grandfather makes eye contact with his uncle. "Big nigger on the bicycle," he says.

His father smiles, and his grandfather notices this and turns his head to face him. Hull knows these men are survivors because they are killers, and they are killers because they are survivors.

When Hull thinks of the voids they've created, he doesn't imagine empty chairs, or empty tables, or empty homes, because those scaffolds, and the lives that may have sprung from the dead, simply do not exist. There's no evidence of them, not even an empty chair, because an empty chair would mean that there is a place in this world for those lives, and there isn't. The chairs are filled with survivors and killers and people like him.

They finish eating, and his grandmother takes a pie from a box and puts it in the oven. Hull collects the plates and stacks them in the sink, and his father tells him to leave them for later. His uncle's new girlfriend dampens a sponge and wipes down the table. She carefully scoops the debris that fell from his grandfather's plate into her palm. Hull can't stop looking at her legs, and where they lead as she bends over.

It's snowing harder outside now, and the crows are gone. The wood fire is still burning, and steam rises from the grill as it melts the snowflakes. His father zips his jacket and steps out the back door to stand beside the flames. His uncle takes a six-pack from the kitchen and walks into the snow with his grandfather.

By the time Hull pulls on his jacket, his father has added three small pieces of cedar to the coals. The air smells like snow and salt water from the bay, and of the dead reeds in the marshes. His father pokes the fire with the blade of a hatchet, and the wood smokes for a moment as though it may be too damp to catch. Then the flames begin to spread across the underside of the wood, and the flakes fall hissing into the brazier.

His grandfather stretches out his hands without the ring on his finger.

"How was the bird, kid?" his father asks.

"Smoky," Hull answers.

"Next time you should brine it," his uncle says.

"Next time I'll let you smoke it," says his father.

"I'd rather do venison. I have this dip with bourbon and molasses."

"The bourbon wouldn't last long with you at the controls."

"See how easy it is to rile up your old man?" his uncle says, and his father smiles and pokes the fire. "You really want to see him riled, though, ask him about that cathouse he used to lay up in when he was stationed in Seoul."

"Go get another log," his father says, and hands him the hatchet.

"Nice Korean massage parlor," his uncle calls after him.

The wind picks up and begins to blow the flakes sideways.

At the woodpile, Hull takes the hatchet and splits another piece of cedar. He watches his hands carefully, conscious of every finger, and feels the downstroke of the axe and holds it the way his father showed him.

Snow blows in through the collar of his jacket as he hunches over to collect the kindling. He hears his grandfather's voice and his uncle's, followed by something low and clipped from his father. When he turns back across the yard, he can barely see them through the storm, clustered together around the fire.

•

He's in history class on the second floor, and the teacher is asking what they've learned from the chapter about Russia. When Hull says, without really noticing that he's spoken up, you should never fight a two-front war, especially east out of Europe, the rest of the students turn around to face him.

He's got his license now, and his uncle is dead in Huế City, and he's been driving his dead uncle's Dodge Charger. The front end does something funny from the accident near Pendleton, but only upward of seventy miles an hour. The teacher was in Europe himself, late in '44, but he was at a desk in France and was only a private. He's maybe ten years younger than Hull's grandfather.

Hull's family has never quite fallen into the lines of American generations. They've always been just a little old or just a little young for whatever war they're fighting.

Hull is big enough and fast enough to make varsity as a sophomore, except he quit football in the fall, and he isn't going out for track next semester. He talks with the teacher after class, and the teacher asks about his grandfather. They know each other a little from the Lion's Club, and the teacher wonders how everyone is holding up, with that gold star in their window.

Hull has been going to the movies on school nights, telling his father he's out at the library. He's been hanging around with another kid, Dave Johnston, who was also a jock once. Johnston played for the baseball team and can throw at a bird in the sky and hit it. He's small and thin, though, and hasn't hit puberty yet, and he's not going to make the team in the spring, and he knows it.

Lately, instead of pitching, he's been working on becoming a beatnik. They met in gym class, and Hull's grades, since the fall, have been slipping. After the movies, they've also been out shooting together—they both know shotguns, and they've been using books from the library for skeet practice.

"Pull," one of them says.

The other spins Tolstoy into the air and screams, "Fire."

"You'll turn it around," the teacher says. "Your father will make sure of it before I do. No one in here had an answer for that question, at least not like the one you gave me. It's in your blood. You'll pull it together."

Hull takes the GT test in the school auditorium on a Saturday morning when he's a senior. His father doesn't know yet that he's been to the recruiter.

The proctor is the same history teacher from his sophomore year, who has a stopwatch and a jar filled with No. 2 pencils. The sections seem improbably short: seven minutes for Automotive Knowledge, eight for General Science, Word Knowledge, and a few others.

Hull's in the room with some of the guys he used to know when he played football. They came in as a group and sit in a cluster. The rest of the space is empty and hollow. There are enough seats for the entire student body but very few people. Hardly anyone is going into the Army anymore, certainly not by choice, and, if they can help it, not straight out of high school.

At first he can hear the football players breathing and coughing and shuffling their booklets. Then he feels like he's alone in the cavern of the auditorium. He's no longer aware of the sounds they make around him— there's just what's on the page and the stopwatch and the instructions from the proctor.

His line scores are high percentile across the board, especially for General Technical and Combat Operations. They route him for more tests for Intelligence and Special Warfare.

In basic, he finds that none of these numbers and bell curves matter. He's too tired to think at first, too tired to do anything but run and crawl, to assemble what they give him to assemble, to repeat what they order him to say, and to sleep wherever and whenever they allow it.

He does find that the guys who do best treat it like a game or some kind of puzzle, like there's something funny and absurd about it, like isolating the pain is as abstract and as ridiculous as walling off a triangle in a rhombus like they're back in some auditorium, deciphering the cutout shapes in the Identifying Objects and Patterns section.

"Don't let that fucking brown round get in your head," they say occasionally about the drill instructor.

They say the same things to each other—when no one else is listening—that he and Johnston used to say after skeet practice with their library books. They talk about girls they want to fuck and how they'd want to do it, guys they hate and how they'd fuck that asshole up, if the law would allow it.

They tell stories about the last time they took a shit in a train station, and what they did when they ran out of toilet paper. Some of them talk about how if they changed this angle, just a little, they might have a better lead on the arc of a target. That's only the best ones, though. Johnston liked that topic—the pitcher in him could go on for a while just on the body mechanics. Now he's somewhere in California.

Hull has tested high enough to go straight into the officer program instead of rotating to Vietnam like the rest of them. He wonders why he went into the Army like his father instead of the Marines like his uncle. It probably wouldn't have mattered how he tested if he was First Marines out of Pendleton. First Marines would've sent him straight to I Corps.

He'll be a little older—like his grandfather, instead of a little younger, like his father—than the rest when he finally makes it to wherever they're fighting, whenever they send him. He'll also be a lieutenant, and they're lining him up for the Q Course.

He spends twenty-three weeks in Georgia at officer candidate school, sitting in classrooms or out in the woods. They teach maneuvering, land navigation, and tactics. They teach sections on confidence, decision-making, projection, and leadership. They're always watching from somewhere, close up or at a distance.

They stand over sand tables and discuss fields of fire. They evaluate response times, problem-solving, communication, stress keys, and emotional stability. They time the class runs with stopwatches. They pit them individually against each other and set up a leaderboard with names and intervals.

Without realizing it, as a group, the class realigns itself. In the mess hall, the alphas eat with alphas, the betas with betas. No one sits with an omega if they can help it. Then they sort the class into teams—fast runners with slow—and run them again.

Each team has to cross the line with all of its members. They expand the course, then shorten it, then make it longer than it's ever been. They add more uphill sections. They run them with their gear and their rifles. They run alongside them, holding the stopwatches.

In small packs, gripping each other's webbing, leaning into each other and pulling, the fast runners become slower, and the slow runners become faster. The splits between first place and last narrow eventually to seconds. They all eat together at the same table.

There's sleep deprivation and exhaustion, and the chaos the instructors manufacture, but there's more time for him to think now. He's conditioned for it—maybe he was made this way and just didn't know it yet in basic. He processes slowly when everyone else is racing, and quickly when everyone else is frozen.

He lies along the ground. The trees are quiet above him. He can hear the wind and the branches creaking. He's selected for semiautomatic. The weapon is loaded with training ammunition. It's late fall and finally cooler.

When they're set up for an ambush and he's listening to the leaves drop and watching the breaks and considering how a stream might funnel a column of his classmates through the valley, he sometimes thinks about deer hunting with his father—his grandfather, his uncle. He thinks about turkey smoked on the grill, the meat brined in molasses and bourbon.

They give him a desk in Panama at the School of the Americas while his application for the Q Course processes. It's 1972, and everyone is saying that East Asia is winding down, that Central America is the next domino.

He's the XO of the weapons depot and spends his days tracking cases of M16s and crates of ammunition. It's his first command, and he triple-checks every ledger. Twice weekly, he directs offloads of material from the States, pallets flown down on C-130s.

The Green Berets on the compound are aloof, wiry, and unshaven. Most of them are so tan, their teeth seem luminescent. He doesn't tell them that he's hoping to rotate back to Bragg if he's accepted. They eat the local food without getting sick and speak Spanish with the cadets, who are shooting and crawling like he was six weeks earlier.

The cadres who rotate through—professional soldiers from Honduras, Nicoya, El Salvador, Peru, Nicaragua—look like they're in costume in their US-made gear and kitted out with weapons from his depot. Their instructors teach them joint command, doctrine, psyops, and irregular warfare. There's a building on the campus with a marble staircase lined with photos of Latin American generals. They're SOA graduates and, in the portraits, are back in their own country's commissar hats and uniforms. They've gone on up the chain at home, he thinks, judging by all their bullshit medals.

He goes out in the Canal Zone at night sometimes and drinks in the port bars and listens to the sailors. They're coming through out of Europe and North Africa with all their different languages. Occasionally he links up with Merchant Marines off freighters in the locks—other officers one night, Kings Pointers.

They take him down into the bowels of the old city, where the streets are crooked and paved with cobblestones. One of them is just finishing his first circumnavigation and needs his sparrow. The sailor is drinking cane alcohol under the needle, tilted back in his chair, at the tattoo parlor. Afterward, the blood seeps through his shirt, spreading thinly across his rib cage. At first, it takes on the thin, sweeping lines of the sparrow.

Hull can't stop watching the stain blot and spread as the sky pinkens. In a brothel called Mi Ranchita, he fucks a mulatta. The sailors take turns with the only white girl in the place, a blonde with dark eyebrows from Eastern Europe.

A rat has bled out on the back staircase from ingesting warfarin. The dawn smells like wet concrete and mosquito pots. He's on a thirty-six-hour pass. The ocean, at this hour, is warmer than the air. He discovers he's standing waist-deep in the shore break in just his dog tags.

There's a civilian named Wells, who picks up packets from the C-130s. He's out sometimes, too, along the waterfront at night or eating in the Balboa American Foreign Legion. He's a little older than Hull and also from Virginia. He says he's in the diplomatic corps. On the airstrip he wears aviator sunglasses. Mostly they talk about Cavaliers football.

Over beers he shows Hull a photo of his wife, a girl with dark hair from an old cotton family. He's hoping to get her rotated down to his next station, probably in El Salvador, maybe in Nicoya, where there's been a military-led revolution. He says he went to Yale and studied José Carlos Mariátegui, Marxism, and Latin American economics. He seems bored most of the time, like he's tired of Panama, or just their conversation.

They drink together anyway, off and on, until Hull gets his orders. They're both waiting to move up, or on, and recognize the anticipation in each other. Before Hull lifts to Bragg, they exchange forwarding addresses.

In North Carolina, the heat and the mud are even thicker than Virginia. It's not as hot as Panama, though, which is almost a blessing. Now there are lessons on the mule as a pack animal, how to delouse their ears, to maintain their feet, which terrain to deploy them in, which breeds are appropriate at which latitudes and elevations. He learns what feed they like, how many light machine guns go in a load, and how to balance them. An imbalanced load puts undue strain on the animal.

The mule withstands hot weather better and is less susceptible to colic and founder than the packhorse. The mule takes better care of itself in the hands of an incompetent driver. The foot of the mule is less subject to disorders. The mule is invariably a good walker. Age and infirmity count less against the mule than the horse.

Under certain conditions, pack bulls can be used to good advantage. The pack bull, with its wide-spreading hoof, can negotiate mud in which the mule, with its small hoof, will bog down or founder. While slower, bulls can carry heavier cargoes than the mules usually found in most small war theaters. Good pack bulls can carry from two hundred to two hundred and fifteen pounds of cargo. They can make about fifteen miles a day loaded. After five days' march, they will require a rest of five to seven days if they are to be kept in good condition. Mixed pack trains of bulls and mules do not operate smoothly due to their different characteristics.

At night, he studies the diagrams of equine and bovine bones, teeth, and musculature—ergot, fetlock joint, pastern, coffin bone. They're organized like the manuals the instructors have provided for American- and Soviet-made weapons, detailing parts, maintenance, uses, and tolerances.

The instructors say he'll know all of this material better—asshole to bridle—if he ever ends up in theater. Maybe him and his donkey will be downrange of a Kalashnikov. First he has to hump his ass across this course.

Physically, it's almost incomprehensible. Basic and OCS were exercises in strengthening inherent weakness. Now, at least initially, they search for whatever weakness is left and exploit it. The goal here is voluntary withdrawal.

If a teammate quits now, the instructors say, it's almost assured he'll quit later on the battlefield. Therefore it's better to eliminate him before he becomes a liability under fire. Voluntary withdrawals are marked *not to return*, and NTRs are sent back their units.

Some guys are tough, but they wash out in the classroom. Others can't apply the classroom to field simulation: The political power and popular support of an opposing force must always be considered. A coordinated reaction requires political and military leaders to recognize that an insurgency exists and to determine its makeup and characteristics. Before most counterinsurgency operations begin, insurgents have seized and exploited the initiative. In these cases, counterinsurgents undertake offensive and defensive operations to regain the initiative and secure the environment.

The immediate cause of intervention usually has been the neglect and repeated refusal of the local government to carry out its obligations. Climactic conditions in the probable theater of operations will affect the organization, clothing, equipment, supplies, health, and especially the operations of the intervening forces. A campaign planned for the dry season may be entirely different from one planned for the rainy season.

A roving patrol is a self-sustaining detachment of a more or less independent nature. It usually operates within an assigned zone and, as a rule, has much freedom of action. Assigned missions generally include a relentless pursuit of guerilla groups, which is to continue until their complete disorganization.

Native officials are usually helpful in securing reliable guides and interpreters. Local inhabitants who have suffered injury from hostile forces, and those having members of their families who have so suffered, often volunteer their services for duty. The integrity of these men must be tested in the field before they can be considered entirely reliable and trustworthy.

Depending on the prevailing conditions, the distances between men within subdivisions of a patrol operating in thickly wooded terrain will be about as follows: point, 10 to 40 yards; advance party, 5 to 20 yards; support, 3 to 10 yards; main body, 2 to 5 yards; rear guard, 2 to 20 yards. The distances between various subdivisions in the column will vary from 10 to 50 yards or more, depending on the strength of the patrol and the nature of the terrain through which it is marching.

Hull is usually on point because of his sense of smell and his eyesight. Some situations, he finds, will require the cutting of trails through wooded terrain. He likes the physicality of it. The lead cutter is charged with direction. In general the trail will follow a compass azimuth with necessary variations as determined by the terrain features, the ease of cutting, and operational security.

As a prerequisite to trail cutting, the patrol leader must have a general knowledge of the area, the direct flow of the more important streamlines and intervening ridgelines, the distance to his objective, and its general direction from the point of origin. One cutter at the head of a small column will suffice. When it is desirable to open a trail for pack animals, there should be three to four cutters.

Supplies transported by air may be delivered by landing or by dropping from the aircraft while in flight at low altitude. To avoid undue loss by breakage, articles to be dropped must have special packing. Skilled personnel can wrap almost any article so that it will not be injured by contact with the ground after being dropped. Explosives, detonators, liquid medicines, etcetera, may be swathed in cotton, plastic, or excelsior and dropped safely. The ideal shape for a drop zone or landing zone is either square or circular.

Before commitment into operational areas, Special Forces detachments prepare for their task of training indigenous forces by developing a tentative instruction program. When committed into a ground war area of operations, required items are delivered with the detachment's automatic supply drop.

Throughout the organization, development, and training phases, combat operations are conducted. With the aid of prior and concurrent psychological operations, the goals of these are to, one, succeed in attracting additional recruits to the indigenous force; two, assist in gaining support from the civilian population; three, give the area command an opportunity to evaluate the training conducted; and four, increase the morale and esprit of the indigenous force. Throughout the training program, constant attention is given to the psychological preparation of the people to accept government support in construction programs and establishing sound local government.

Situations may develop where the known leader of the resistance movement is of such importance or caliber that a senior Special Forces officer and a more complex staff will be required to effect the necessary coordination and future development of the force. At this time, a B or C Detachment may be chosen for infiltration.

It is important to understand the distinction between design and planning. While both activities seek to formulate ways to bring about preferable futures, they are cognitively different. Planning applies established procedures to solve a largely understood problem within an accepted framework. Design inquires into the nature of a problem to conceive a framework for solving that problem. When situations do not conform to established frames of reference, planning alone is inadequate, and design then becomes essential.

Hull has already been to Panama and has picked up some of the language. He's assigned Spanish in Phase II as his focus. There's more attrition in the culture and language section than in the phases of jump school, and search and evasion. Other students have trouble with advanced interrogation and MOS training. Mostly these are mental mistakes, not physical.

After two years, he seems taller and leaner. He spends a month planning for the incursion of a fictional country in North Carolina. He has a map that details more than a dozen rural counties. He has a set of objectives and radio frequencies. In the dark he jumps from the tail ramp of a C-130.

He lands near a grove of pine trees and packs his canopy. He knows there's no live ammunition out there, but his legs are shaking—all of the instructors playing the opposing forces know all of the tricks he's spent two years learning.

He meets the guerilla chief at a rendezvous point five miles from the drop zone. The G chief only speaks with him in Spanish and is played by a master sergeant from Oregon. The G chief was in Laos in '64, before they sent him to Panama. The G chief never breaks character—he only tells Hull where he's from and where he's been, after the exercise ends, two weeks later.

For now, they concentrate on training a cadre, which is played by a group of underclassmen from The Citadel. They succeed in the ongoing disruption of the supply lines within their district.

They give him his beret and long tags at graduation. He gets a Seventh Group challenge coin down in Central America, which is the size of a half-dollar and should always be kept on his person, except during operations.

The coin cannot be defaced for ease of carrying, such as drilling an eyehole to accommodate a lanyard. It has a cluster of arrows on the tail and reads *Anyplace, Anytime, Anything* in English. The face motto, *De oppresso liber*, is in Latin and comes from St. Augustine. *Corripiendi sunt inquieti, oppressi liberandi*. The turbulent have to be corrected, the oppressed to be liberated.

He forgets his coin one night when he's out with his team in the Canal Zone. They're tapping theirs lightly on the table, and he's the only guy without one. He has to buy drinks for the rest of the night, starting with boilermakers.

Of course they know he's SF, and of course they know which group he's in—they're on his fucking A team and don't need him to pass a coin check to prove he's a brother. He's a fucking new guy, though, and FNGs require lessons in protocol.

They do a few long-range patrols in Guatemala, along the Mexican border. There are so many guerilla fronts and counterinsurgency cells, that it's hard to keep track of them. Graduates of the School of the Americas are engaged on both sides of the conflict. The Mano Blanco has been running disappearances, backed by US training and funding. Everything has been escalating for years, though, spinning beyond the control of the American handlers. Now even the CIA has started calling the Mano Blanco an apparatus of state-sponsored terror.

The massacres are larger and more overt, and the opposition groups have responded by targeting high-level officials. The communists have been shooting and bombing in the cities and, in the countryside, digging into the populace. The US ambassador was even killed a few years back, shot a block out from the embassy in the capital. The fighting has been ongoing since 1960, and almost everyone is exhausted.

Hull inserts into a lull, and they mostly do observation and recon in the Xolchiché Mountains. The Guerilla Army of the Poor has organized the local Maya into a social base, which is spreading outward from the Ixil Triangle.

Hull's team is attached to elements of the MNL government's paramilitary, but they cut the Guatemalans out of most operations. The local division commander—a thin politician, whom the Green Berets nickname Pinche Perro—isn't interested in outreach with the Maya, much less in learning their languages. Pinche Perro wants to burn them out instead of engaging psyops to turn the populace.

In the villages, they do some water filtration, pamphlet distribution, and disarmament. When they run out of Betadine, command air-drops charcoal filters. Hull and half the team get cholera anyway, and they lift back to Panama.

He watches the ceiling fan in the infirmary, his arm hooked to a bag of lactate. He thinks about the Maya, who couldn't fly out and who have the same lightning roiling through their intestines. He knows they'll get sick and stay sick until they die or, by some turn of their genes, get better.

When he's on his knees in the latrine, he tries to imagine what it would be like to keep doing this until there's nothing left to shit out or vomit. He tries to imagine what it would be like to know he's going to be down on the pyre soon, behind the village, with the others. He thinks about how, until this century, this is the way most Americans died too—maybe not from cholera, but from some other communicable disease or sickness.

In his family, they have so many stories about the dead in the Revolution, in the Civil and Indian Wars, in the Big One—his great-uncles, their second cousins, lines of the tree that have since ended. No one told stories about his ancestors who were killed by dirty water.

They send his team back to Guatemala, in the south, where they're now running weapons for the Contras through Honduras into Nicaragua. He spends a few hours in Nicoya, tracking a Sandinista cadre that's been operating hit-and-run raids across the border. They pack weapons caches into duckboats and onto mule trains and run them across rivers and over mountains. One afternoon, they exchange fifteen seconds of gunfire with a group, which may or may not consist of narcos, in a pass on the Pacific side of Costa Rica.

Each team pulls back and repositions itself, waiting for nightfall. They all want to go on their separate ways, but they don't trust each other enough to move without the cover of darkness. It's the first time he's been in contact, and the effect on his senses is a lot like the pills they eat before night ops.

In the late sunlight, he can see every crease in the rock face layered by geologic era. The birds above him each have a distinct song isolated from the background rustle of the wind in the canopy. He can hear the narcos on the far side of the trail whispering and, under their sweat, smell the soap they washed with three days earlier. The scent is antiseptic, like the cleaning solution on the floors in a bodega somewhere—the place where he buys six-packs of Balboa beer in Panama City.

•

The house in Virginia seems smaller than he remembers. The hardwood floors are a deeper color and more vibrant under their topcoat. He doesn't like walking across them for some reason. They seem too beautiful to be stepped on, even though for most of life, he never even noticed them.

It's the first time he's slept in his childhood bedroom since he came home from basic training. His parents have changed the furniture and pulled down the cutouts he tacked up from old magazines. They've painted over everything except in some places he can still see the pinholes in the drywall.

They've saved his stuff in a box somewhere in the attic, but he can't be bothered to go up and sit in the cold and sort through it. He'd only find pictures of Dodge Chargers, and maybe a few of Sonny Jurgensen after Sonny came over from Philly to play for the Redskins.

They've kept his high school yearbook on the bookshelf. Otherwise the room is plain now and sterile, like all spare bedrooms that once belonged to someone's children. The land seems emptier and quieter, and the house looks even smaller from the outside, viewed from the edge of the field, its windows glowing in the dusk in the distance. It's November, and he can see his breath dissipating in small clouds of condensation.

The barn owls are out, scanning the tall grass for mice and rabbits. One banks as it passes, turning its white face and black eyes to look directly at him. It's only a few feet overhead, and he turns with his own eyes and his own face to track it. It's soundless as it climbs in an arc, trimming its wings. Then it's out hunting over the fields again, a wheeling shadow.

He follows a game trail the next morning. There's frost on the uncut hay and, it seems like, frost on his father. His father is out front—has always been out front—but Hull has to stop occasionally to wait for him to add some distance. If they each kept walking at their own pace, they'd just bunch together.

His father's hair is gray now, and his skin seems pale except Hull can't tell if that's only because his own skin is so much darker. It's the first time he's noticed that he outweighs his father. It's not that his father's old, really. It's just that it's been a while since Hull has seen him.

It's been a while since he's walked with anyone who isn't specialized to set pace, carrying their own bodyweight in gear if needed. Hull actually feels so light in his down vest that it's like he's forgotten something. He's only got his deer rifle and a few rounds in his pocket. He keeps checking along his belt for the Colt pistol that isn't there, and patting his chest for a map and a compass.

The wind switches when they stop to drink some water. Now they're upwind from the deer, and they're going to have to circle around to come in from another direction.

"Hey, bud," his father says before they start out. "You okay with another mile?"

"You want to rest? You want a little more water first?"

"I've got a bottle of Black Label waiting in the pickup."

Someone is burning wood in a stove somewhere.

They cross the next field faster than Hull expected. In a dell they skirt a pasture that's empty but fenced for cattle.

"You remember that one Uncle Pete used to tell?" Hull says. "About the bull? And the drunk who hog-ties him?"

"What was the punch line?"

"I don't remember. Something racial. Something about the drunk thinking the bull was a guy on a bicycle."

"When did he tell it?"

"I don't know. At Thanksgiving once."

His father stops and they listen for a while.

Eventually, they see a buck in the distance. It's obscured down in some trees and way out of range for a .308 shot. The wind switches again, and they're on their way back to the pickup.

"He would tell something like that at the table."

"He brought a girl home that day from California," Hull says.

"I don't remember."

"Mom and Grandma seemed to like her."

"I think that joke was actually your grandfather's."

"You're right, I think."

"It's funny," his father says. "Your uncle was so much younger than me, I hardly remember him once he grew up. I guess he didn't last long grown up, anyway."

When they get back to the house, his mother is setting out the chairs and the plates at the table, one for each of them, just three now in the warmth of the kitchen.

Part II

Fight

11

THEY CAME on dirt bikes and quads, in mud-caked cars that bottomed out on the graded road, their mufflers striking boulders and dragging through puddles. Some drove rusted pickup trucks and parked beside the concrete coliseum, gathering in the lot as the sky grew thin and high overhead, almost white as its color dissolved and then deepened into darkness.

The men wore wide-brimmed hats made of straw, their hands calloused and stained with grease and earth and fish blood. Some shared guaro, which they sipped from plastic bags while others waited for the jefe's men to unload pallets of beer, filling the lot with talk and laughter as their children ran in the dust.

The handlers, whose truck beds held cages made from chicken wire, shouted to clear a path through the crowd, lowering their dogs into the dirt near the arena's side door, where Emilio stood waiting in his rubber apron. A group of policemen aided in the work, drawing their clubs to hold back a line of drunks and gamblers. The officers formed a half circle around the doorway, the shoulder boards on their uniforms touching, until each animal had disappeared into the tunnel. Then they retired to a corner of the lot to lean against their motorbikes.

Ellis photographed the slant of their belts, unscrewed his 200mm, and knelt to search through his backpack. When he found the 50mm, he attached it to the camera and thought of his fish-eye lens on the shelf in his apartment, and the images he might have shot now if he had brought it.

He waded into the crowd, walking almost as if he were sliding his feet through the dust. His body felt leaner than it had before, tall and pale among the locals, yet he never felt overtly present, a trait all the best photographers he knew seemed to possess.

12

HULL MET the two men in the Prado at the arena and sent them back to the compound. The driver handed over a roll of money and a thin navy booklet embossed with an eagle and faded gold lettering.

Hull tucked the photographer's passport into his back pocket and counted the cash—six hundred and fifty American. He divided the bills and handed them back to the men.

"*Bien hecho,*" he said. "*Descansen. Y envien de vuelta el próximo equipo.*"

As the truck turned out of the lot, he checked the photographer's position in the crowd at the foot of the stadium. For a moment, Ellis was there—then he was no longer visible. Then his arm extended toward the sky, and his hand aimed a camera down at the heads of the locals.

He fixed the location using the flash and shifted his attention to the policemen under the tree. One of the officers saluted with two fingers, and Hull shook his head, and the Nicoyan went back to observing the photographer.

Hull's knees cracked as he walked to the far side of the arena, his joints swollen like a door that had been warped by humidity and no longer fit into its frame. The imprecision in his legs bothered him the most in the small moments when he realized he had become accustomed to every injury he had received, and the compensations he had developed to adjust to the pain.

He stretched forward from the neck to keep moving like he had when he was younger, and admitted nothing made him feel as strong as he once was. He also knew his injuries were now visible—affecting his timing, eroding the confidences in his brain, reminding him of things of which he was no longer capable. He tried to convince himself that some of the pain would pass after the rain. He could sense another storm forming, somewhere over the mountains.

He entered the door and descended through the hallway, past the room filled with dogs, their voices amplified by the concrete. He climbed a ramp that led out to the base of the stands to meet the three men he had assigned to mirror the photographer.

The coliseum was quiet, and one of the men was smoking a cigarette. All of them seemed anxious and were dressed in jeans and thin collared shirts with fake pearl buttons.

They looked like the rest of the men from the town nearby. They all had been born there, and they would have been farmers or fisherman if the jefe had never come west from the Caribbean.

"*Qué pasa?*" Hull said.

"*Nada,*" the team leader answered, and Hull smelled cordite, or the memory of cordite, and thought of a counterinsurgency team which he'd trained to eliminate a FARC cadre in Columbia.

Half of them were dead in the first six months of the operation. They had also once been farmers.

"*Sola una noche,*" Hull said. "*Un gringo solo. Pero mucho dinero.*"

They all laughed, and he handed each man a Motorola receiver, which they tucked into the waistbands of their jeans. He stood back and helped them run a set of wires up through their collars and into their sleeves. They fit the speakers in their ears and clipped the microphones to their cuffs.

"*Tú eres Ojos Uno,*" he said, and pointed to the team leader. "This is just like we covered in training."

"Okay. *Claro.*"

"*Ojos Dos. Y tú Ojos Tres.* Understand?"

They nodded.

"Now switch to channel five."

"*Más despacio por favor,*" the team leader said. "*Nuestro* English *es malo.*"

"Remember what I told you on the phone today and what we covered in the classroom," Hull said slowly. "Stay high in the stands." He swept the stadium, pantomiming with his hands. "I want you where there's good visibility. Eyes One, you're roving." He made a walking motion with his fingers. "Eyes Two, you're on the east side of the building. *El este.* Eyes Three, the west side. *El oeste.* Bring him to me after the last fight. *La última lucha. Ojos Uno,* that's your job, *tu trabajo.* Make sure you get his camera. I'll meet you downstairs when it's time."

13

THE RANGE Rover cut through a puddle and came up on the far side with its wipers streaking the glass. The jefe shifted in his seat to look back at Padaratz and the American girl who had said she was from California. He smiled when he saw Padaratz's hand on her thigh. She looked familiar to him in the same way that all American beauty was familiar—vacant and artificial.

"Tell me something," he said to her.

Her backlit eyes seemed manufactured, like the spun green glass in marbles.

"Did you know that when you got on this man's plane this morning, you would be flying here with the best dog breeder in Brazil?"

"Come on now," Padaratz said, removing his hand from her leg.

"No, it is true," the jefe said.

He unbuckled his seat belt so he could directly face them.

"This man spends his whole life making interest from his father's bank," he continued. "He goes to school with the Americans to learn more about banking so he can help his *padre* someday. Then he spends the next thirty years breeding dogs in the favelas. I should have never introduced him to my father. Now he might know more than my father did about breeding once, maybe, what do you think, Jairo?"

"Your father knew many things," Padaratz said. "Some of them I'll never know."

"I'm not so sure," the jefe said to tease him. "You write sometimes for the *Game Dog Times*. I think very little is lost in translation. However, no, I think you know more about filas and campeiro bulls than anyone on this planet."

"Thank you, my friend."

"It is true."

The jefe gripped the handlebar above his head, swaying in rhythm with the truck.

"You should see the way he can look at them and know what needs to be added or subtracted," he said to the girl. "From their blood, I mean. He has an eye for which are brave and which are *cobardes*, and then he finds the right bitch, always. I'll never know how.

"Tell me," he said to Padaratz, "this animal I hear you have brought today, he is a mix of a fila mastiff and a dogo with some pit terrier. How much does he weigh? They tell me he is lean but big."

"You have been talking to your Emilio," Padaratz said. "Or your Mr. Hull. All I can tell you is that when we dropped him off this afternoon, I saw your mestizo and I think my fila might be a match. That *chucho* of yours is too young, Janvion."

"Yes?" the jefe said. "Emilio does not think so. We will see. My scatter bred did not have to fly today or ride with Mr. Hull. He views every time we drive anywhere as a problem. He thinks they all need to be solved. Sometimes I think he drives too fast. Sometimes I think he lacks a real education. Maybe your fila might be carsick."

"Or airsick," Padaratz said, and laughed.

"I like to drive fast," the girl said, and the jefe swung his gaze toward her.

He blinked, his lids closing over the broken capillaries.

"Have you ever been to a dogfight before, *hermosa*?" he asked, and reached back to touch her knee. "Wait, don't answer that. Remind me to ask you again later. First I want to know how you and my friend here met."

The girl sat up quickly and recrossed her legs and smoothed her short dress.

The jefe looked down between her knees, at the shadow that ran up her thighs under her hem.

She smiled again when she saw that even the driver was watching her in the rearview mirror.

"I guess I met Jairo at Ibirapuera Park," she said, looking to Padaratz.

"Oh yes?"

"During fashion week. We've been together, what? Almost six months."

"You are a model, then."

"I'm a textile buyer."

"Well, you are pretty enough to be a model."

"Thank you."

"It is true."

The girl glanced down at her legs.

"I like it better this way," she said. "I can go to the steak house, if I want, with Jairo. I don't have to feel too guilty about that."

"You live in California?"

"I grew up in San Diego, but I actually live in Rio. I've been there for almost eight months."

"Oh yes?"

"Yeah. It's great. I really like it."

"*Fala Português?*"

"*Falo um poco.*"

"She's working very hard," Padaratz said.

"Very nice. So why did you pick to live in Brazil?"

"I love the culture," she said. "I'm actually half Brazilian."

"Oh yes?"

"Yeah. On my father's side. He moved up to LA when he was eighteen, I think. That's where he met my mom. She's part Filipino and part Japanese. So I guess I'm sort of a mutt."

"What's that?" the jefe said, pulling at his lower lip.

The girl raised her voice over the engine.

"I said I'm part Brazilian and part Filipino and part Japanese."

"So where is your American?" the jefe asked, and the girl squinted through her marble eyes.

She was very tan and had small, bleached specks on her teeth even whiter than the rest of the enamel.

"I'm sorry?" she said.

"If you are half Filipino and half from Brazil, how much of America is in your blood?"

"No, no. I'm a quarter Filipino, a quarter—"

"No. Yes. I understand. I am just wondering how American you are."

"Janvion, be nice to her."

"I am," the jefe said.

He extracted his eyedropper and applied the solution. "I am only teasing. So have you ever been to the fashion week in New York?"

"Yeah," the girl said. "It was huge."

The jefe wiped the saline from his cheeks.

"How old are you?"

"Twenty-four."

"You look much younger. How old were we, Jairo, when we went to the city?"

"Twenty-one. It was our last year in school."

"I enjoyed New York very much."

"I sort of thought it was dirty," the girl said.

"Oh yes?"

"All the guys just talked about money."

"Yes," the jefe said. "That can be very boring."

At a rise in the track, the jungle thinned and the ocean came into view, purple and orange in the sunset. Then the trees whipped past, casting the truck in darkness, and the driver switched on the headlights, the truck descending into the valley.

14

HULL UNLOCKED the side entrance to the arena and waited for the jefe's driver to jog around the Range Rover. Mud had fanned back along the length of the truck, and the man opened the rear door carefully to keep it from brushing his suit jacket. Then he stood aside as the girl unfolded her legs from the back seat and took his arm.

She checked the ground as she stepped out in her heels, her hand brushing a bit of the mud on the doorframe, causing her to rub her fingers together.

At the airport earlier, she had seemed intrigued when she'd heard that Hull was an American expatriate. She had frowned, just like now, when he told her it was only by necessity.

"This way, please, Ms. Souza," Hull said, and gestured for her to step inside as Padaratz climbed out behind her. Then he led them partway into the concrete hallway and returned to the entrance.

Checking the lot, he saw only flies and leaves and the deepening blue of nightfall. He could hear the muffled noise of the crowd on the far side of the arena, where the clearing had been cut back enough so the only place to set up an ambush was from within the tree line.

One man with a .338 could cover most of the valley, he knew, but he had also instructed the drivers to park very close to the wall, minimizing the distance between one door and the other. A good marksman might be able to align the gap if they timed it correctly. A sniper might also try to hit the jefe while he was still in the Range Rover, except the doors were armored and the windows tempered, and a shot through glass was always indefinite.

His father had told him once that anything was possible in a firefight. He had found that to be almost accurate. The solution was to plan for what was most likely, at least initially.

"We're clear," Hull said, and the jefe paused, one foot still in the truck, to retrieve a pair of rubber sandals from the floor mat. Then he dropped them onto the ground and stepped into them, rubbing his swollen eyelids.

He looked like he often did to Hull—as if he'd been sleeping.

"Mr. Hull," he said as they entered the hallway, "everything is ready? So tell me, *hermosa*, you forgot to remind me to ask you. Have you ever been to a dogfight?"

"No," the girl said. "I told Jairo that I didn't really think I wanted to come."

"That is understandable."

"But he took me to the last bullfight of the season in March, in Mexico City, and I loved that, so he says this isn't that different."

"What did you like?" the jefe asked.

"I thought their clothes were beautiful."

"I have the bulls here sometimes. It is very special."

Hull closed the door behind them, and they made their way to the kennels. He lifted his arm to speak into his sleeve and remembered that the reception was always broken in the tunnel. He looked at his watch to estimate the time it would take for the surveillance team to deliver the Prado to the next guard shift—a round trip of thirty-five minutes.

He counted silently, in time with the throbbing in his knees, and decided that the gates could be opened at seven. There would be three fresh men to cover the box by then, not including himself and the driver, a total of eight armed men in the arena with Padaratz, the jefe, and the girl, plus the photographer.

"It is a little different from the corridas," the jefe was saying, his voice echoing out ahead of them. "I admire the bravery it takes for the bull and the man. One, he has to have it in his blood. And the other, he holds it in his brain, maybe in his blood as well. It takes something in the way of fortitude to not run when you know you should run. However, they are not evenly matched. Nothing is an even match for a man who has other men working for him, and who has spent his life studying how to become a master of a certain skill set. And also training with the tools to do so."

"I wouldn't know about that," the girl said.

"You will like it, I think," Padaratz interrupted. "It is like what you have seen before, and you love me and I love my dogs. You will love it."

The jefe ignored this.

"You do know about that, *hermosa*," he said to the girl. "You saw the corrida. How did it end?"

"They killed the bull."

"Yes. They killed the bull—the cuadrilla, the picadors with their lances and horses, the toreros. You will see animals here that are much more evenly matched."

Hull opened the door at the end of the tunnel, and the training room was even louder now with the handlers hunched over their crates, speaking to their dogs and feeding them dried beef through the chicken wire. The jefe lingered in the doorway. Then he shook hands with Emilio, who had come forward in his apron, and the rest of the party filed into the room behind him, and the men inside lined up to greet him.

The girl placed one foot carefully in front of the other, her eyes trained on the floor like she was walking through a room in the dark. Hull came up behind her and touched her on the elbow and pointed to the opposite door. Her hand still carried some of the mud from the truck, he noticed, and he thought of his ex-wife, her fingers pressing dimples into the soil at the base of their dogwood trees.

At the top of the ramp, they entered the arena, where the night hung above the stands, the metal halide lamps shining on the dirt of the ruedo and the depression at its center. He moved ahead of the group and mounted a short flight of steps, climbing as quickly as his legs would allow him, and unlocked the door to the jefe's box, which was a walled platform set apart from the stands, its seats covered by an awning.

They entered and sat on a couch while the driver offered them a bucket of ice and bottles. The jefe opened a beer and handed it to Padaratz. Then he opened one for himself and gave the girl an imported water from Iceland.

She held the bottle, her pupils dilated despite the lights.

"Would you like some wine, *hermosa*?" the jefe asked, and she shook her head and stared at Hull as he spoke into his sleeve.

"*Cinco minutos*," a voice told Hull over the Prado's engine.

Hull dried his neck with a handkerchief and tapped the driver on the shoulder. "Do you have your weapon?" he asked, and the man pointed to a bulge under his jacket. "Wait here."

At six minutes past seven, the announcer arrived, followed by the three guards in the Prado. Hull escorted them inside and checked their positions, then went back into the tunnel and descended the ramp to the kennels and opened the side door for the vendors and the dancers.

On the radio, he gave his men a final set of instructions.

"*Están listos?*"

"*Momentito.*"

"Switch to channel five," he said, and climbed the steps toward the jefe's box. "Keep the safeties selected on your weapons."

Two of them split off to open the main gate, walking on their young legs toward the arch.

•

The public address system crackled across the lot, issuing Spanish through the static. Ellis tucked his camera beside his ribs, covering it with both of his hands, and slipped sideways into crush of bodies, moving toward the arena. He passed a group of children eating sticks of cane sugar and stood up on his toes to see a bottleneck at the gate ahead of him. Then someone pushed against his backpack, and he inched forward, driven by the weight of the crowd.

He tried to slide backwards as two men with Kalashnikovs opened the entrance, and the first wave of people entered the gate. He looked to the policemen, who were mounting their dirt bikes and speaking into their radios, the crowd continuing to surge, and was carried into the gangway, where the ghosts of halide filaments glowed against his eyelids.

In the center of the ruedo, a percussion line was performing—boys in uniform, the girls in skirts and headdresses with flamingo feathers strung into their hair. He raised his camera and shot a frame, the plumes drained of color under the artificial light. Then he photographed a toddler being led by the hand of her mother.

He smelled cooked meat and lowered his camera and found a man with a platter of skewers. He shot another image of a group of girls, in cheap dresses and makeup, purchasing beer from a collective of vendors. When someone whistled, he turned in the direction of the sound and saw the box containing the jefe.

"Come up for a minute," the jefe shouted from the top of the wall, and Ellis looked into his bloodshot eyes—and across at Hull, who was speaking quietly into his sleeve. He crossed to the base of the parapet, following the curve of the stands to a space where, overhead, a blue-and-white awning flapped gently in the breeze, brilliant in contrast to the dirt of the ruedo.

He climbed the steps and paused before he entered the doorway, nodding at a man and woman. The couple seemed rich and almost alien in their European clothing. They sat holding their drinks, watching him.

"It is a nice evening," the jefe said. "Sit down. Would you like a beer? We have Aguila *o* Dorada. *Bien fría*. We also have some water. This is don

Padaratz and this is Ms. Souza. This is Mr. Ellis. He is here visiting from Los Estados."

The jefe reached into the bucket and gave Ellis a beer without waiting for him to answer or offer his preference. The other man acknowledged him without offering his hand.

Ellis looked at the girl and took a sip of his drink and saw the city, the hot sidewalks in the summer, remembering how the air conditioning would seep from the storefronts and how sometimes, after shooting with Kara last August, they would stand together in the shade of an awning, drinking from a bag, sweating in the cool pocket of a doorway.

The jefe took him by the arm and gently turned him so they both faced outward over the parapet.

"Tonight there are five fights," he said. "The last one is between a special dog I have prepared with Emilio, and a special dog that has come with Mr. Padaratz. I think you met my animal last night. This one is the most important. The most decisive."

"I was thinking about shooting some of it from a low angle," he said.

"*En el ruedo?*" the jefe said. "That would be very dramatic. Go wherever you like, I think."

He found his saline and rolled his eyes until they were almost blank, lengthening his mouth, stretching his face.

"After you are finished," he said, "Mr. Hull will pay you and drive you to the airport."

"I'm on a flight tonight? What about the photos?"

"You can give me your film."

"I'm shooting digital."

"I forgot this."

"I can leave you my memory card. Or I can send a file transfer."

"I am certain this will work," the jefe said, and applied the saline. "You can give your card to Mr. Hull before the airport. He will have the package with your payment. I'll remind myself to remind him."

"I need to go back to the house for my passport," Ellis said, and the jefe extended his hand, his eyes still wet and bloodshot.

"It has been a pleasure to meet you," he said. "I enjoyed discussing photography. I agree with you now, I think, about Mr. Cartier-Bresson. He was a talented man, and I think you are also talented. You should go now and see what you can see, and shoot what you can shoot before they start the first fight."

15

HULL FOLLOWED the photographer's flash and checked the position of his men in the stands.

In the box, he could smell the machine oil from his Sig Sauer, along with the earthen odor that wafted up from the ruedo.

He turned back to the strobe, which flashed like the heat lightning in the sky the night he rode with the Salvadoran troops to a ranch at the edge of the capital—the officers lining the men up in firing rows, the sergeants staking the cattle in the field, the cows rolling their eyes.

The advisers from the embassy had been speaking quietly in English.

"They've been stocking up here?" the colonel asked.

"Yes sir," Greenview said. "According to Caceres."

"Have you tried to set an ambush?"

"There's some kind of compromise, sir. The FMNL cadres close to the city never try to secure assets at this location when we're in position."

"So if you can't keep them from drinking, you turn off the tap."

"Yes sir."

"What's your command policy, Captain?"

"To adapt to the conditions on the ground, sir," Greenview said.

"This might be outside your mandate. In my opinion it's bordering on total war."

"Not quite, sir, at least according to battalion."

"You went to the Academy. You've read your von Clausewitz."

"Of course, sir, but it's civil war, sir. And remember Sherman."

"Captain Hull," the colonel said. "Make sure their own officers and NCOs deliver the orders. I want to be off-site when this goes down. We're taking an element of the convoy back into the city."

Hull waited, but there were no other instructions. He called to Claros and relayed the orders, turning away from the rest of the men.

Overhead, the lightning flickered.

The sergeants had brought out the owner of the ranch, who had begun to pray as they made him kneel among his cattle.

"I think I will win tonight," the jefe said, and stood up from the couch to stand beside Hull at the parapet. "I think my animals will win, and I think we will also have a good result with the photographer and the Zetas."

·

They carried wooden planks up the ramp, the edges pre-chiseled with dovetail joints. Each knelt and assembled the boards around the sunken patch of earth at the center of the ruedo—faint blue veins running across Emilio's hands, a boy with one eye closed as he supported the weight of the wood, his tongue visible in the corner of his mouth.

Ellis shot a single frame of the empty pit when they were finished, and trailed them through his viewfinder to the tunnel. Then he blew dust from his lens mount and, framing a sequence of Emilio on the ramp with the boy, looked into the crowd for whomever Hull might have speaking with through the wire.

When the announcer's voice echoed through the arena's speakers, Ellis turned to see a man come from the direction of the jefe's awning. The official held a cluster of tapered sticks in one hand and a small metal rod in the other. He was dressed like the rest of the men in the crowd, except his hat was made of suede instead of straw.

Nodding into the stands, he climbed into the pit and pointed back to the tunnel, where Emilio reappeared along with another man, each holding a dog by the collar. The animals scrambled low to the ground, slavering and pulling against their leads, excited and terrified by the noise above them.

A knot of gamblers in the front row rose to their feet to watch them pass, the money in their hands cropped by the top edge of the frame. Under the halides, the coat of the jefe's pit bull shifted from gray to silver while the town dog, which was heavily scarred, seemed to absorb the light and appeared to be limping.

Ellis positioned them along the bottom of his viewfinder and continued to shoot, edging toward the pit as Emilio hefted the animals into galvanized tubs to wash them. The boy, who had helped to assemble the box, returned and directed the pit bulls toward a scale beside the basins.

As the animals were weighed, the boy wrote the readings on an index card, then climbed a staircase to a booth at the top of the arena.

"*El perro del jefe,*" the announcer said. "*Del don Janvion Garcia, pesa veinticuatro kilos y medio. El perro del señor Miguel Herrera, veintitrés punto siete.*"

The gamblers became louder with this new information, and bookmakers came and passed out tickets, writing quickly with pencils.

Ellis switched back to his 200mm and adjusted the aperture on Emilio and the other handler as they placed their dogs into the pit. The official with the suede hat also stepped inside the box now, and he gave each of the handlers one of his tapered sticks.

Kneeling, the man inspected the dogs, using a bar to pry open their jaws, then flicked his metal rod on opposite sides of the box to score scratch lines into the earth.

Ellis switched the drive mode to a high-frame rate and engaged the flash, his strobe lighting the dogs' eyes—dead white and glowing at their centers. He shifted for a clearer line of sight and drew his elbows in beside his ribs.

The dogs reared onto their hind legs and snapped at the air as the handlers squatted over their hips to control them. The official walked to the center of the pit, relaying instructions in Spanish, looking first at one corner, then at the other as the crowd became silent.

Ellis brought the camera to his face, and his flash flickered. He depressed the shutter as the handlers dropped their leads, and the animals crossed the pit, their tongues pulled back alongside their cheeks, their wet teeth lucent and flitting in his viewfinder.

Initially, the fight reminded him of dogs wrestling in the snow, the animals nipping and spinning in circles. Then a drop of blood fell into the dust and caught the light under the halides and was trampled in the dirt, and the two pit bulls stood back on their hind legs, quiet except for a whining in their breathing, their teeth chipping against each other.

He focused the 200mm on the ridges of their hackles and shortened the exposure and could not keep his hands from shaking. The animals rolled for nearly a minute before the jefe's pit bull seized the town dog's jowl and shook, its spine bending away from its hips in an S, increasing the violence of the motion.

He shot a sequence of the tear itself, the inner tissue brightly sterile for an instant before it rimmed with blood. He pulled his face away from the viewfinder and remembered a photo he had exposed of a man on a stretcher—the soldier bleeding from his face as he held a pen to write his signature on a waiver. In his mind, he saw the Marines turning back into the valley in Afghanistan, even after their friend had almost been killed in the poppies, while he wondered about their fear and how it felt without the layer of camera glass to separate them from the danger.

He had known, even then, that he never wanted to photograph combat again.

Now he swung the 200mm toward the box under the colored awning and brought the jefe into focus. In the magnification from the lens, it appeared as if he was not watching the dogs at all—instead, he was standing at the parapet, looking directly into the camera.

At the center of the ruedo, the town dog began panting heavily, its cheek now stripped, the cartilage along its muzzle shining waxen in places. As the animal attempted to slink back toward its handler, the jefe's pit bull leapt again and clamped its foreleg, and Ellis lit the moment with a strobe—the white fibers within the torn calf, one dog backing away as the other, its spine rigid, pushed forward. Then the pit bull tore through all that was soft in the limb, and bore down until the bone shattered.

Ellis was still shooting when the animal was rolled onto its shoulders and had its neck torn out in the dirt. His final photo captured the jefe's pit bull, its muzzle and chest slick with blood, looking expectantly toward Emilio. In the background, the other handler was holding a pistol, a small splinter of silver.

He turned to run as the sound of the first shot cut across the stadium.

·

Hull pulled the jefe away from the parapet and pressed one hand against his Sig Sauer. A shape moved in his peripheral vision, trailing the scent of the girl's hair. He grabbed her and pressed her down onto the couch and measured the pause between two additional gunshots.

Something tightened in his back, and he adjusted by leaning forward from his neck. Pressing with his other hand, harder now than he intended, he applied pressure to the girl's shoulder to keep her from standing.

Across the ruedo, men were pointing down at the pit, screaming and tearing their money back from the bookmakers, women already climbing the staircases, pulling their children by the elbow.

"*Hijo de puta*," the jefe said, smiling. "That *chingado* has just shot my dog. He shot his mongrel first and removed it of its misery, which is a shame, actually. This is an illustration of how you never know what they will do—people, I mean—when they lose something."

Hull spoke just loud enough to be heard over the crowd.

"Sit down," he said to the girl. "Stay there. Step back from the wall, please, Mr. Padaratz."

In the ruedo, the guards with the Kalashnikovs closed in an arc around the handler.

"No," Hull said into his sleeve. "No, no. *No disparen.*"

The handler's pistol glinted under the halides.

"*No disparen*," he said again.

"*Levante las manos*," they screamed, and the handler blinked inside the pit, his face and shoulders slack, and looked at the guards and down at his hands like someone who had been sleepwalking.

The jefe's pit bull lay in a growing circle of blood at his feet.

"*No disparen*," Hull repeated into the wire.

Then the guards sighted down the lengths of their barrels, and the handler dropped the pistol, and they kicked it away and stepped over the walls of the pit to push him onto his knees.

"*Échenlo, Llévenlo por la puerta principal*," Hull said, and rekeyed the microphone in his sleeve and was stepped on by another transmission.

"*Dónde está el fotógrafo?*" asked the leader of the surveillance team.

The jefe was in his other ear, shouting to the girl, "This man, who is unfortunately a peasant, was a little excited. He is in a lot of debt."

"*No se.*"

"And it was not us who disappointed him, it was his dog."

"*No lo tiene?*"

"He is not shooting at us."

"No, no. *Ojos tres?*"

"So sit down and stay, please, *hermosa.*"

"*No tengo mierda.*"

"He has ruined this fight, but the next will be very exciting."

"Mr. Hull?"

"She is fine."

"We should leave."

"Sit down, Jairo. We still have your dogo coming."

"Fan out," Hull said. "Close the exits. Check the stands. Meet me in the parking lot in three minutes if you don't find him."

His knees ground like glass as he ran for the staircase.

•

Ellis pressed his back against the wall of the tunnel, the third gunshot echoing through the arena, and turned to watch the hallway and the ramp where it opened into the ruedo. He found himself staring at a thin pool of water at the base of the walls, waiting for something to move behind him. He crouched and saw the alley outside of his apartment in the deep winter—a man on his fire escape, hunched in the snow, looking into his window.

A shadow crossed the mouth of the tunnel. He continued down the hall, splashing the puddle underfoot, the drops spreading darkly across his legs.

In the training room, he lowered his head and walked quickly past the handlers and the dogs, which were waiting beside the kennels. Then he reached the hallway and tightened the straps of his backpack and began to run again, listening for footsteps behind him, hearing only the whining of the animals and one of the men speaking to his dog in Spanish.

Outside, he jogged along the outer wall into the rows of vehicles and passed a truck with its door ajar, the interior light illuminating a couple in the cab, the woman's hips rising and falling over the man beneath her. Then he stopped short in front of three men who were leaning against the arena, smoking in the light filtering down from the halides.

They stared at him in silence, their dirt bikes resting behind them on kickstands.

"*Qué onda*," one of them said. "*Qué onda, gringo?*" he added, and the other two chuckled.

Ellis tucked his camera between his legs and unclasped his watch and held it out in front of him.

"*Por tu moto*," he said, looking over to the oil-spattered chassis, the engine wires wound in electrical tape.

"*Qué es esto?*"

"Rolex."

"*Un* Rolex?"

"*De verdad*," he said, and the smallest man in the group leaned forward to inspect his face and made a small shrug and opened his hand.

When Ellis gave him the watch, he flipped it over, rubbing the band and the dial.

"*Y la cámara?*" he asked.

"My camera?"

"*Sí.*"

"*Solo el* watch."

The cherry on his cigarette blossomed.

"*Bueno*," he said after a moment, still shrewd and unsmiling. "*De acuerdo.*"

•

Hull climbed to the west side of the stadium and searched for his men in the crowd, then directed the guards with Kalashnikovs to seal the exits and descended toward the tunnel, fighting against the horde on the staircases.

"*Salgan a la calle ahora,*" he said at the base of the stands, and lost the signal from the wire.

In the hallway, he found sneaker prints leading through the puddles into the kennels and followed them down into the pits, where a handler gestured with his head toward the exit.

Under the sky, a woman in a truck was rising and falling with her hips, and a few men beside the wall were smoking when he passed them.

He paused and listened to their conversation and drew his Sig Sauer, which convinced them to produce the Rolex. He was in the Cherokee five minutes later, bound for the beach house, watching for the photographer on a dirt bike in the headlights ahead of him.

16

THE CEILING fan in the kitchen filled the silence, the pull chain ticking in its housing. Ellis stared into the empty safe and dumped his luggage onto the floor and rooted through his clothing, searching for his passport. Above him, the hollow scrape of the puppy's claws resonated through the door to the bedroom. He unzipped his jacket and went through each pocket, in the process, sliding his laptop into his backpack.

"I'm coming," he said to the puppy. "Quiet for a second. Lie down."

In the bedroom, he lifted her and tucked her into his duffel bag, then searched the mattress and the bathroom for his documents, compulsively glancing through the windows at the road that led up the valley from the arena.

The puppy squirmed against his ribs, and he tightened the sling over his shoulder. Then he left the house and remounted the bike and kicked the ignition. He turned off the headlight as he rode, the moon casting the trees and the dirt track in silver, the light falling across the puddles and the palm leaves, nearly white to almost black.

He was still watching the mirrors when a flicker of color at the edges of his vision made him brake suddenly beside a pulperia.

He sat in the intersection, watching the jungle, an advertisement shining above the door of the restaurant—*CERVEZA BIEN FRIA*—in glowing red-and-yellow plastic.

The shadows in the trees moved ahead of him, a light that was not from the moon or the sign.

"Fuck," he whispered, and slipped the clutch and walked the bike to the far side of the road, pulling in close to the wall, and shut off the engine.

In the quiet, a truck accelerated over the unpaved road.

At first, the sound seemed to be moving away from him, but the light in the trees shifted, and the engine came forward steadily. Then the jungle went dark, and a Jeep emerged from the trees with its headlights switched off and passed onto the beach road in a cloud of dust, a solitary figure behind the wheel, a silver profile.

•

Hull shifted into neutral and allowed the truck to roll downhill toward the beach house. At the bottom of the grade, he used the hand brake to slow his momentum and parked in the same place he had the previous night in the rain. He drew the slide back on his pistol, just enough to check for the bullet in the chamber, and tapped the magazine with the heel of his hand to be sure it was seated in the well.

Sitting, he watched the house and the lights behind its windows. Then he stepped out of the Cherokee and jogged up the track to the driveway, hunched over slightly, pausing from time to time to listen.

On the back patio, he opened the kitchen door and stepped over the scattered clothing on the tiles. He checked the blind spot behind the entrance and moved smoothly into an open space between the sink and the counter. Across the room, the wall safe hung open on its hinges.

He squatted to examine the cardboard box upstairs and a puddle of shit on the bedroom floor and checked the closets and searched under the bed, processing this new information. A drowned tick, full of blood, lay in the drain in the shower. He opened a window and swung his legs out onto the corrugated tin roof and followed the rain gutters to the front of the house, where the walls below him would support his weight.

He stared down from the eaves above the front door at the two sets of tire tracks in the driveway and reached for his cell phone.

When he had been young, but not that young, after El Salvador and the hospital, he had sat with his wife on a roof near a river in Canada. They poured drinks and watched three moose come through the pines.

The air smelled of fresh water and old leaves, and in the bedroom in the rental cottage, he lay on his back in the cool sheets and felt her moving above him. He had cooked dinner afterward and thought of how clear the sky had been and of the long limbs of the moose, and of his wife's eyes.

Watching the tree line, he told himself the day had been beautiful, and knew that this was only an observation, not a feeling, and that the beauty of those moments had simply passed through him and left nothing behind. The change in him then was recent enough that he still knew the day should have left him feeling long and relaxed and tired. He had already returned to the restaurant so many times in his mind, however, that he could no longer imagine himself without the scars on his legs or the memory of Claros bleeding from his jugular.

"You're go for encryption," the tech from Dallas said.

"I've lost contain on the photographer."

"Is his phone on?"

"I need you to relay that information."

"We should have uploaded GPS. Hey, man, wake up."

"Put me on speaker," Hull said.

"What do you know about hacking cell towers? the tech from Dallas asked.

"I haven't drawn a Voronoi sketch since San Quintín," said the one from Houston.

"Hull's on speaker."

"Okay."

"He's lost the photographer."

"Okay."

"He wants us to triangulate."

"Is the target phone on?"

"No."

"Then that's a problem."

"Can you hack the cell towers?" Hull asked, and there was a shuffling noise as they covered the microphone.

"Yeah," the one from Houston said finally. "If his phone was on right now, we could probably upload a GPS package. We have his cell ID numbers already, his ESN and his MIN. We actually could have given him something that would have turned his phone on without him knowing while he was down at the house."

"Only discuss contingencies that are still applicable," Hull said. "Can you hack the towers?"

"It might take some time, about ten hours, but the TDMA and GSM grids are both vulnerable. The problem is if he doesn't have his phone on, there's no point."

"What are our other options?"

"Well," the one from Dallas said, and took a breath. "There are his credit cards and his bank account, and that girl in Morocco. And his father in New York. We can use them and set up a tree and watch them online, and whoever else we get by cross-referencing commonalities in contacts. I'm assuming we don't have hardware or eyes-on surveillance, unless you have assets in those locations."

"There are no assets in place," Hull said.

"We can maybe add his editor. We can also hack his voicemail. We don't need his phone to be on for that, and any other targeted voicemail, depending on the network security. So if he lets them know where he is, he lets us know. We're in his email, too, obviously. If he logs in to pretty much anything that's part of his footprint, anywhere, we can backtrack him to an IP address."

"Keep me updated on your progress," Hull said, and climbed back in through the window.

17

ELLIS WATCHED his mirrors throughout the night. He saw only darkness behind him, and the bike made good time, and he pushed the engine and switched on the headlight as he rode. He grew wet in the mist that settled in places over the track. He stopped at the edge of a ditch when it was very late, and unpacked the puppy and waited while she squatted.

Circling first, lying in the dust, she refused to drink the water he poured into his hands, and looked up at him with her blue eye, panting. She continued to watch as he stepped from the embankment and moved away from her. Then he unbuttoned his pants and also squatted.

She was resting her chin on her foreleg when he whistled to her softly. He could feel her coughing inside of the pouch as he remounted the bike.

At dawn, he crossed a plain dotted with conacaste trees and cattle, which stood in a field checkered by fence lines. He braked near a gate that separated the highway from an unpaved turnout, and scanned toward the mountains. He unzipped the duffel bag, and the dog licked his fingers, moving against his ribs, her nostrils flaring toward the breeze.

Iberia lay to the north, the airport an hour away at most. The length of the Ocaña Peninsula stretched away to the south. No roads ran eastward into the mountains, at least as far as he could see. Somewhere to the west, he knew Hull was waiting in the Cherokee, if he wasn't already ahead of him, at the airport.

He revved the engine in the pink light and turned south, the concrete running smooth and black through the fields.

•

If Hull felt anything at all about the photographer, it was a faint distaste, not for his decision to run but for the implications of that choice for both of them. In the dark he left the beach house and switched on his high beams, following the tread marks in the track.

He pulled up a map on his cell phone and scrolled across the expanse of the jungle, zooming in to consider the network of unpaved roads and the highway to the east. He turned on the air conditioning and felt his wife's hand on his wrist, a memory from before El Salvador, her fingertips cool, her mouth counting quietly.

"Your heart beats fifteen times less per minute than mine does," she had said.

He braked and stepped out into an intersection east of the coast and studied his own tire tracks, where the Cherokee had come from the valley. He squatted and looked across at the pulperia and read the photographer's sneaker prints under the glow from the sign.

"Son of a bitch," he whispered.

He lost the trail not far inland and followed the most obvious track eastward for a while, searching for headlights. Then he backtracked, shutting the engine off occasionally so he could listen beside the track.

He turned onto a fire road that ran up into the hills, and parked on a ridge with a view of the valley and stood on the roof of the Cherokee, surveying the jungle in the moonlight, watching the small breaks that the tracks made in the canopy.

It was after eleven, according to the clock on the dashboard, when he turned back for the arena. A Daihatsu pickup truck sat in the lot, the only vehicle still remaining from the town.

He parked on the south side of the building, near a garbage ramp, which was covered by storm doors. The jefe's Range Rover was pulled in close to the entrance to the tunnel, its engine running.

He depressed the buzzer at the side door and waited under the camera for the click of the lock. Emilio opened the passage and led him into the training room, where it was oddly quiet.

"*Dónde está el jefe?*" Hull asked.

"*En el ruedo,*" Emilio said, and Hull turned for the opposite door toward the ramp.

In the tunnel, he passed the boy from town, who was dragging the jefe's scatter-bred animal, the body trailing blood over the concrete. Hull crossed the ruedo to the base of the stands, where he found the jefe with the surveillance team—the three men standing uncomfortably in the first row with the handler from the first fight sitting between them.

"Mr. Hull," the jefe said, touching him on the shoulder. "Where is Mr. Ellis? These men told me you have misplaced him."

"Go wait in the car," Padaratz said to the girl.

"I think you should go with her, too, Jairo," the jefe said, and applied saline to his eyes, and Padaratz took the girl by the arm and led her into the tunnel. "I could barely watch his dogo against my scatter bred in the last fight. It was finished in two minutes. Have you seen Emilio? He worked very hard on that animal. I'm sure he isn't happy. Wait, tell me first, where is the photographer?"

"He's somewhere in the next valley. He's most likely moving east."

"So he is outside of your containment?"

"He might try to go south to the international hub in San Quintín. He might try the airport in Iberia. It's closer, and he's familiar with the location."

"This is interesting."

"We have his passport and his money. Unfortunately he did access a vehicle."

"And this is a problem?"

"I'd like to move a team into Iberia. You have an asset there we've used before, and I'm going to call the Nicaraguan border. I also have my techs trying to penetrate his hardware, and I'll see what else I can do between now and the morning."

"You can bring him back?"

"We can deny him options. I'll send out two men on the quads tonight. He could break down somewhere between here and the highway, which is another way of saying we might get lucky. The team in the Prado's already trying to move out ahead of him. The terrain presents a challenge. Our access to vehicles is limited. You control the police and the towns here and to the east. If he moves through any of those locations, we'll hear about it. Right now, I'd advise investing in an offer that can send the locals out tonight with a directive to look for an American on a dirt bike. Or at least make it worth it for them to put it on the wire that we'd like to hear about it if they see him. Whichever channel they use, we have to make sure it isn't monitored by the OIF. Twelve, twenty-four, forty-eight hours out, the highway and the scenarios it presents narrow at a certain point to a limited amount of exits."

"This sounds thorough," the jefe said. "It sounds like you are being thorough. Now I also would like you to have a word with this man who has shot my animal. These men know him, you understand this, so they cannot do it. Regardless, he ruined the first fight, and I liked that pit bull. His name was Chispa."

"Does he speak English?" Hull asked, and looked over at the handler.

In his stained jeans and fake pearl buttons, the man could have remained a farmer. Instead, he had become a gambler and a dog breeder who had fought his animals against the jefe's and rarely won.

"He won't need to. Not for this conversation," the jefe said, and Hull felt the weight of the Sig Sauer in his waistband, its metal edges digging into his hip.

He pressed his forearm against the grip to keep it from shifting, making sure the jefe could not circle around behind him. He thought of the rows of dogwood trees in bloom at the base of his driveway.

"*Tú*," he said to the handler. "*Una palabra por favor.*"

The man stood and adjusted his shirt, smoothing it across his chest, which had been soiled when the surveillance team searched him in the dirt.

Hull waited until he climbed down into the ruedo before he took a step back and drew his Sig Sauer. Then he shot the handler three times in the chest.

He advanced and fired again, still careful not to turn away from the jefe.

Looking up from the small spasms in the handler's legs, he aimed for the center of his forehead and fired a final round and rolled the body into a tarpaulin with Emilio's help and carried it through the storm doors and placed it into the back of the Cherokee.

The wooden sensation in his joints returned as he drove it out to a mangrove. Sometime near dawn, he showered in the guesthouse and shaved and charged his phone.

He called his men in the Prado, instructing them to move south toward Cárdenas. He slept for an hour and packed the Browning shotgun into a bag along with a Kevlar vest, two shirts, and a mixed case of buckshot and slug loads. In the kitchen, he oiled his pistol. Then he attached a set of local license plates to the Cherokee and drove south to find the photographer.

North

Ellis

●

ROBERT CAN'T watch the things the nurses do with her dressings. He can't watch them uncoil the lengths of gauze that, just a day earlier, they spent all afternoon packing into her. He can't watch them rewrap her open sores and clean her plastic tubing. He's not supposed to watch. He's only nine, and his father tells him to go outside when the nurses come every day at three thirty.

So it's fine, he tells himself, that he can't lean in her doorway and keep her company. If he's not supposed to stare at the scars, where the doctors have gone into her stomach and tried to cut out the cancer, it's okay that he's outside now under the sun, by the bay, watching the clouds run past and the seagulls bobbing in the marina.

It doesn't matter that he feels better as soon as he's at the shoreline, and the roof of the house falls behind the bulrushes. He doesn't want to be able to look up to the second floor anymore and imagine her in the bed at the foot of the window.

He'll skip stones for an hour, feeling the strength in his arm, and his own life, and the reflection of the sun on the water, coursing through him. He'll go back before dark when the nurses will be gone, and she'll be hooked to the wide bore needle again, sleeping.

He'll eat dinner in the kitchen—soup from a can and Ritz crackers. Maybe his father has been out while the nurses were in, and brought back sandwiches. His father used to go to the deli and get them turkey-and-salami heros dressed with oil and vinegar. The rolls were so packed with meat, he used to have to press everything back into them with a fork to flatten them out, to stuff the toppings back in before he could eat them. Now his father usually forgets to eat. He looks so much more tired and older than he did in the beginning.

If they give her enough medicine, she might sleep until his father has to change her bags at two in the morning. It'll be dark soon, and they'll watch television together, maybe the show his father likes about the birds in the Serengeti. They won't have to look at her at all now for a few hours.

If there's enough medicine in the bag, and if they can each get to sleep soon, Robert won't have to look at her again until tomorrow. She'll still be dying in the house, and he'll still live there too—and there will only be so much they can hide from him, and only so many places he can hide from what's happening in his parents' bedroom. But if she stays asleep for long enough, maybe he can make it through the night, then slip out for school without having to go in there and see her.

The packing is clean and bright when the nurses unwind it and coil it into her. It's brown and wet when they pull it out, though, using nothing but tweezers. They sit on stainless-steel stools, snaking it down into the red pails they keep between their knees, working on opposite sides of the new bed, which they moved in for her a few weeks earlier. It seems like there are always stains on the sheets now, too, and on the inside of her gown, along with the brown fluid soaked into the swaddling.

It's been sunny and warm all spring, and he's at the window at the end of the hall, not watching them hum and talk to each other as they wash her with sponges. She doesn't like when they lift her naked and transfer her onto the gurney. She doesn't like all the wrapping and rewrapping.

At least, he thinks, she's only moaning today instead of screaming. At least they didn't have to carry her all the way to the bathroom today, trailing some kind of slurry.

He's heard them explain to his father why the incisions will no longer close like they did after the first few surgeries. They go all the way through, as far as he can tell, and they keep spilling over with something that smells like spoiled milk and acid. The liquid runs onto the bed and across the floor once it's seeped through all of the bandages. The nurses keep coming back to clean it up, changing out all her soaked fabric, swabbing the floors with mops and antiseptic.

It was easier when she was still in the hospital—they could still go home at the end of the day and leave her. Now he can't decide what he wants to see at night when he closes his eyes—an image of his mother waiting in the bed the next morning, or his father at the bottom of the stairs, waiting to tell him she's gone finally, gone already.

She's only forty-five, which seems old to him because everyone seems old to him if they're more than twenty. Everyone keeps saying how young she is and that this shouldn't happen to good families. He doesn't know how to feel about the idea that he wants her gone, finally, and that he wants this over already.

She's sitting up in the bed now, drinking water through a tube that's longer than it should be. She's so weak that she's having trouble drawing the water out from the cup, which is set on the tray at her waist. She's having a good day otherwise, and she's smiling and keeps looking up at the April sunlight cast from the window onto the ceiling.

He comes in from the doorway and picks up the cup, then adjusts the tray so that all she has to do is suck a little, and everything flows easily.

"Hi, kid," she says.

"Hi, Mom."

"Don't ask me how I'm feeling."

"You look happy."

"It's a nice morning."

"I'm home from school already, Mom. It's the afternoon."

"Well, what'd you learn today?"

"I don't know. Nothing."

She looks away from him to the wall, where there are framed drawings from when her hands were still steady. She had a long, easy way of sketching. There's a lobby she designed in the city, with high ceilings and marble. There's a house she did for a client in Greenwich.

She's told him this before—and he understands she's just trying to leave him something to remember—but he doesn't want to hear about how hard she worked in school to become an architect. He doesn't want to hear about how, if she felt better, she'd take him to the Met, or about how groundbreaking Zaha Hadid's exhibit was in the '80s at MoMA.

Until a year ago they used to live near the park and the museums, so it was easy to walk to all of them. Now they live in a house with a yard near the water. On the wall there's another drawing of a stream and a copse of trees that was drawn by her father. She's hung it in a place that doesn't get much sunlight—she's trying to keep the colors from fading any further.

He doesn't want to hear about how light can fall across a room and highlight or distort its elements. He likes how his mother can make him see things, sometimes from a place he's never considered, except now he just wants to see her get up and walk around a little.

He knows he's done something to her with the question about school and his answer. It still smells like acid in the room, and spoiled milk, and antiseptic. He notices, as if it wasn't there earlier, a plate on the tray of sliced apple. It seems like more than a year since they left Manhattan.

It's been a long time since she sat up in the bed and was quiet enough to discuss anything. She seems to be in one of those places, which she reaches sometimes, between the medicine and the pain, where she resembles the mother he remembers. She's not there completely, and he knows she never will be again, but right now she's at least a shadow of who she was before the cancer.

His father has told him that soon even this piece of her will be a memory. They both—all three of them—need to make the most of these moments before that happens.

Now maybe he does want to hear about the light and the room and its elements. Maybe they can sit and leaf through one of her heavy books of Le Corbusier or Koolhaas. The smell of the ink and the expensive paper has always and always will remind him of her. Maybe he does want to hear about how her father and her father's father came from a lineage of designers and draftsmen in England. She's told him that her grandfather worked on the Flatiron Building as an architect in some capacity, but they've never been able to find his name anywhere in the records.

"You're getting big," she says.

The straw has slipped down onto her chest, and she's licking her lips now. He lifts the tube without touching her through the gown and sets it into her mouth.

He holds his breath while he's standing close to her. She's panting a little and finished drinking.

"Dad's been picking me up from school at lot," he says.

"He's been home lately?"

"Yeah. Is he going to get fired?"

"Don't worry about him, sweetie. He knows what he's doing."

"How are you feeling?"

"I bet you guys are having fun together."

"He's a pretty bad driver."

"Oh god."

"He almost backed into Lyla's dad in the parking lot."

"He grew up in Queens. The driver's seat's a foreign object."

"We had a car in the city."

"Except he never drove it. I always drove when we went camping. Remember?"

"I remember."

"Do you remember going up to my cousin's all those weekends?"

"Yeah. It was beautiful. And quiet."

"You know that's where my father grew up."

"I know, Mom."

"Hey."

"What is it?"

"Nothing. I just want to look at you."

"You want me to get you something to read?"

"No, I'm going to rest for a while. What time is it?"

"I don't know. Almost three thirty."

"Hey."

"What is it?"

"How are you doing in your classes?"

"They're fine, Mom."

"Make sure you study."

"Okay, Mom."

"Someday you're going to want to get out of here. You can't do that unless you have options."

"Dad says you were the one who wanted to move here in the first place."

"I have some friends who have kids the same age as you. I grew up out here. I wanted you to experience it."

"I don't hang out with most of them."

"You will someday. They all know you."

"I like how we're near the water."

"I had a feeling you would."

"I miss our apartment too."

"You're doing great."

"When did you first move?"

"For college."

"I feel like everyone is so quiet when they come over."

"They know I'm resting."

"I feel like I'm different than the other kids."

"You know, I was one of the only women in my class at architecture school. And then the only one at the firm who wasn't a secretary."

"What was that like?"

"It was like knowing everyone is looking at you. And then having them treat you like you're invisible."

"It feels like people are watching us now."

"They just know I left. And they know I came back. Most of them have been here forever."

"They never left?"

"Maybe for college. Then they came back again."

"They know you're sick."

"They know I don't feel well."

"Scott's mom brought us ziti."

"That was nice of her."

"It wasn't good."

"But you guys ate it?"

"Yeah. We ate it."

"Tell her it was delicious, okay, when you bring the dish back to her?"

"Okay, Mom."

"You've always been good, Robert."

"This is where you tell me to always be myself."

"Exactly," she says, and smiles.

"It seems easier to be like the rest of them."

The light has come down from the ceiling. It's in the corner on the stream and on the trees drawn by his grandfather. The paper is so thin and faded that he can see through it in the beam like a skin of parchment. Where the pigment is weak and discolored, he can see the backboard of the frame and the dark heads of the screws, which are sunk into the wood to hold the slats together.

"You can be whoever you want, Robert. Except I want you to remember that most people aren't thinking about things like you are. Most people just go through life and want what's easy. And that's all they think about."

"This isn't easy," he says.

"I know, sweetie. It'll be over soon."

"Then what?"

"Then you'll see there are things happening in this world. You'll get big. You'll want to go be a part of them."

•

He's at a bus station in Maryland, and it's early, and there's frost on the pavement. He's a little hungry and cold and has been riding Greyhounds for most of the weekend. It's the second time in a month that he's told his father he's sleeping at Ryan Sheehan's. Sheehan usually tells his parents they're visiting his brother in Brooklyn.

They've been using public transportation for trips like this lately, even though Sheehan's parents gave him an Audi A6 for Christmas. The buses and trains force them to stop and see places they otherwise wouldn't.

They've already nailed a few shots on this trip, especially at the terminal in Baltimore, which would have been impossible if they'd driven. He takes Sheehan's Leica and steps into the road for a minute. He likes his own camera, too, but a Leica's a Leica.

He's just milling around, hoping to see something. They're in a town called Elkton, maybe fifty miles south of Philadelphia, probably twenty miles south of Wilmington. It's pale, and it's Sunday, and there's almost no else one on Main Street. By this afternoon, they'll be at the Port Authority in Manhattan, close to Penn Station, where they can get the train back to Long Island.

He shoots a few frames of an old woman on a bench drinking coffee and eating a pastry. Her face, or maybe it's just the way she's sitting, isn't that interesting. He doesn't want to use all of the film that Sheehan loaded. He also wants to shoot something worth keeping.

He stops at the side door of a diner and watches the line cooks and dishwashers in the kitchen. He finds an old license plate on the next block over. It's lying in the gutter along with a newspaper blown open to the classified section. The two objects are lying too far apart to get into the same frame, so he uses his sneaker to push them together.

He exposes a few shots, moves the paper some more, and then looks back at the bus station. The old woman is standing now and pouring out her coffee onto the sidewalk. Her body is bent and delicate as she finishes and shuffles into the terminal. He only gets a single frame of her walking away from the puddle. Eventually, though, a crow lands and hops into the liquid. It stands on one leg at a time in the steam to keep its feet from burning.

He can't figure out what it's pecking at, or even what it's doing, until he remembers she was also eating something. The crow finishes the rest of her pastry, then perches on a streetlamp.

It's raining the next morning, but there's clear sky to the south and tall, backlit cirrus on the horizon. He's in calculus, staring out at the clouds, which sort of look like a range of mountains. He's reading *National Geographic*, or leafing through it, mostly for the images. He likes the classic layout and how they give the photos room to breathe, especially compared with *Outside* and *Traveler*.

He's been thinking about the crow since yesterday. Now he keeps going back to a series of landscapes shot in a port town on the Kamchatka Peninsula.

In his favorite image, the harbor is ringed with fishing trawlers and panelák buildings. The man-made elements are all pushed to the bottom of the frame, almost to the waterline, and seem weighed down by the sky and the descending layers of snow, crags, and mountains.

They've been talking about Ansel Adams in his seventh period photography class, and he likes the idea of being outside again, in the rain, with his camera. Overall he's bored with Adams, but he's also fascinated with his technical perfection. His Yosemite images in particular are so still and sharp that it seems like everything must have been quiet and motionless when he shot them.

The photos he's been making of the bay and the bulrushes always seem chaotic. The water always seems to be roiled with current, and there's always the evidence of wind or something else, which he can't quite identify, shifting across his subjects.

His best photos seem to be of animals and people, mostly when they won't sit still or aren't aware of him to begin with. He knows Adams worked with nature because he was trying to say something about preserving it. Robert feels like he'll never find this kind of message or purpose.

He's tired of shooting his friends smoking joints and cigarettes. He's tired of the basement parties at their parents' houses. On most weekends, he seems to end up walking down their endless driveways, then climbing their iron gates to find somewhere to sit without all that light and music. He's even tired of watching these two girls he knows drop ecstasy and make out with their eyes half open and their pupils dilated.

The first few times he saw them kiss, he was rolling, too, and he went home and thought about their lips and their tongues while he masturbated. Now he can't seem to focus on anything except for how they always seem to stop, then pull back to look around the room to see who's watching. Everyone's figured out that they're not bi or anything. They're just doing it for the attention. He can actually sit near them again during the week and look at the backs of their heads without getting hard in AP English.

He expected this point of his life to feel more urgent, maybe like Larry

Clark's *Tulsa* series. It's funny when he thinks about how most of the people in those images—doing speed, half dressed with their thin, beautiful bodies, lost in their tragic and American youths—are now his father's age.

He wonders how many of them are dead or never made it as far as his mother. He feels like his photography—which is more like David Alan Harvey's anyway, in style but not in subject—is missing something that Clark's isn't. Maybe it's the desperation. His friends kind of know that everything, no matter how much they fuck up, will be easy. They're all going to get old like Clark did, like everyone does, and be just like their parents, though that seems pretty distant.

He's enrolled to go away to school in September. He's already been riding the train into the city, and not just to catch the Greyhounds with Sheehan. He's been walking through Manhattan with Naomi Olsen, just shooting. Naomi was a senior last year, but now she's a freshman at Columbia.

She's never been into photography—she's thinking about majoring in political science—but she writes song lyrics. They can't figure out why some of their friends went to school up in Connecticut or New England. They can't figure out why some of them joined frats or sororities, or why they hung around with them in the first place.

They're underage in a bar in the Village. They're feeding goldfish to the turtles, which are swimming along the back wall in an aquarium. The fish cost a quarter a piece or five for a dollar. The bartender keeps giving them away for free as long as they keep ordering tall boys of Pabst Blue Ribbon.

Naomi has fed more of them into the tank than he has. Her roommate is away for the weekend, she tells him.

In September he expects everyone to be better than he is. Most of them have been to prep schools or private schools with better visual arts departments. Either that, or they've all done well in all the same contests. He's never had the courage to enter most of them. Some, he's never even heard of.

One of his professors is with Magnum and has worked with *Vanity Fair* and *The New Yorker*. He expects their first assignment to be about something manual—a technical exercise using a function of the camera. Instead, they're sent out to shoot only a specific color. The instructor wants red this week, then purple. He wants narrative elements that can be associated with the tone in their subject matter.

For red, Robert shoots the glazed ducks and the neon characters in a butcher shop in Chinatown. The images are a little technically sloppy in their focal emphasis. The butcher on the other side of the window is interesting. The glare on the glass is distracting. The Cantonese writing, glowing red, does nice things for the tonality.

"We've seen other photos like it," the instructor says. "It's a cool image, though, and it shows some talent."

He walks up to the emergency room at Bellevue for purple. Around midnight he shoots a woman who has been in a car accident. She's sitting alone along the wall, filling out the forms for inpatients. Instead of upset, she mostly looks angry. Her hands are shaking and her leg is bobbing. Her knee is cut and three of her fingers are swollen. She's having trouble holding the clipboard.

She doesn't notice he's taken her portrait. He's moving from one end of the room to get the angle and the bruises. He doesn't want to stop and have someone see him. He doesn't want to deal with security. The movement this creates, the instructor says in the next critique, conveys plenty on both sides of the lens, all that chaos.

In the rest of the critique, they discuss a few technically perfect skylines and sunsets. There's a girl in her underwear on a blanket in an apartment. One guy has shot graffiti washed out by the violet light in the subway. His classmates, for the first few weeks, have been friendly but distant. Now they go out of their way to talk to him.

Between the instructors and the rest of them, there seems to be some kind of consensus. Not all of them like his images. There's a girl in Visualization and Composition who always shreds his submissions. He sometimes struggles in the studio and with technical lighting. He isn't the *best* photographer in the class. He's really fucking good though. He also knows how to take the instruction and keeps getting better.

He's in a crowded place off Bleecker Street. The table and the floor are wet from the beer they're spilling. They're talking about the ability to anticipate an image before making the exposure. They're talking about the photographic system and the influences it has on the process. They're talking about how you can choose to highlight or minimize the camera's distortions. They're talking about the subjective nature of consciousness.

They all take a photo from their respective sides of the table. Some of them use the fill flash, which is blinding, and the bartender sends over the bouncer.

The next place is even more crowded, but the girls are from NYU and way hotter. They're in black pants or short skirts and makeup. They seem to be into a table of stockbrokers in the corner.

"How's that for subjective?" someone says.

"My dad, I think," he says, "wanted me to be an architect."

"My parents gave up on me a long time ago."

"No, he's rad. He's into this. It's just I think he thought I'd be more like my mother."

Lately, it seems like the images he wants to shoot and the things he needs to make them—all the light and the subjects, the places he needs to stand, the moments he needs to be there—have just been lining up in front of him.

He runs into the girl from Visualization and Composition as he's walking back to his apartment. She's drunk, too, and smoking a cigarette. She's wearing a vintage T-shirt with a silk screen—the album cover of Joy Division's *Unknown Pleasures*. Later, when he comes, he's looking at her eyelashes.

He's in the darkroom, and the darkroom stays open until four in the morning. He's a junior and working on a project for Advanced Black-and-White Printing. He's been juggling his color work between the assignments for this class and the course loads for Wet Plate Collodion I and Digital Imaging.

Within the curriculum, he's spread across more than a century. It feels like, depending on which camera he chooses, he can see from the present into history. He can look at the images he's making and understand how they were made in the 1860s. He can jump forward a hundred years, then another thirty. In the latter span alone, the textures change—in ways he can feel but can't describe—between Kodak film and Fujifilm. He can load a roll of Kodachrome X, then Velvia 50. He can shoot them and sit in the darkroom and compare them in the emulsions. He likes the smell of the chemicals and, in the red light, the sense of anticipation.

Every frame he shoots on digital arrives in an instant. The results make him adjust in real time to each subsequent exposure. He isn't sure how he feels about the influence overall, but it's useful. It's like he's learning in fast-forward.

Across the range, it seems like every tool and technique feeds off the other. His instructors keep hammering the idea that technical mastery breeds confidence, and confidence breeds creativity. Some of them repeat it so much, it's like they haven't realized he's figured this out now—he understands it intuitively.

It's snowing and the bars are closing when he comes down from the darkroom. He's carrying three cameras, a file full of prints, and keeps slipping in his sneakers. He passes a few kids he recognizes from Alternative Process outside of the Blue & Gold Tavern. They're all scheduled for darkroom time the following evening.

He stops and talks with them about who they saw out tonight and what they've been shooting. He's got a few okay ones, he says, of a kid and his mother in the rain outside of the Flatiron Building.

He tries to be quiet when he unlocks his door, because his roommates are sleeping. He sets his stuff down in the dark, takes off his wet socks, and opens the fridge and eats some cereal. His professor from Advanced Editorial has helped him submit a few RAW files to the *New York Times*, the *Wall Street Journal*, *Esquire*, and *Newsweek*. He checks his email, but he hasn't heard back from any of them. The shot he wants them to print is from Union Square station—a soldier in his helmet, filing through a turnstile filled with commuters.

He wasn't even in Manhattan when the planes hit in September. He was out on Long Island for the last week before the semester started. He spent most of the morning on his cell phone, trying to reach his father. He remembers how quiet it was in the backyard without any air traffic. Eventually his father just showed up at the house, covered in dust, still carrying the mask he'd made from a coffee filter. His father knew plenty of the guys who'd worked in the towers, he said. He walked all the way across the Brooklyn Bridge with one of them, starting from Wall Street.

When Robert thinks about that day, mostly he thinks about how it felt to be an orphan for those ten hours. He also thinks about how he never even picked up his camera. Even once he was back in Manhattan, he stayed away from the pile. Instead, he's tried to document how much has changed since then. To him the solider is about the small things they've lost—with his rifle and gas mask in the subway. Maybe *small* isn't the right word, he thinks. Maybe there is no single word for it.

In the spring the photo editor at *Esquire* emails him back about the woman at Bellevue. They can't run the shot, because he never had her sign a release, but they need an intern, and they like the stuff he keeps sending. He sits in a cube with an old Macintosh desktop and clicks and drags through the slush pile. Mostly the submissions are burned onto CDs, but there's also a light table. He's in charge of packing and mailing the slide sheets back to the contributors. The CDs, he's been told, can go into the garbage.

He starts to see the kind of range the editors want in a submission. If they haven't commissioned you, or they don't know you, they want about fifteen or twenty photos total. They want you to show them you can self-edit and curate. The last thing they want is for you to shoot a whole card, burn it onto a disk, and send it.

He wouldn't have gotten the job if they didn't know his professor. He helps light a few cover shoots and watches and listens as they cull through images. He learns that if you find someone who likes your stuff, you should focus there first, rather than scattering your submissions. Part of getting published is having someone else who's also willing to publish you. No matter what, everything you send in needs to make them stop and look for at least a few seconds. Otherwise they'll just start ignoring you, too, like everyone else coming in over the transom.

Eventually they let him shoot a few fill shots around the city when they need something specific for editorial. He gets a full-page vertical his last month there and gets drunk with another intern to celebrate. It's a photo of a kid sitting in front of a bodega in Brooklyn. It's dark out and the sidewalk is crowded and the kid is thin and kind of feral. He's under the awning in a pool of light, just watching everything pass, contemplating his prospects. They run it to illustrate a piece of short fiction by some writer he's never heard of.

He graduates and rolls the internship into freelance work. A few of the photo editors he knows have branched out through Hearst or gone to other groups like Condé Nast, or other magazines. One girl, who isn't much older than he is, will actually email him if they're looking for something specific. She's an assistant photo editor and has started to ask him to either cover what he can for them or to go check his files, then pull an image.

He gets a few spread photos, and they hook him up with some writers who are working on features. The first time he gets a check big enough to cover his utilities, he sits there, staring at it for a while, turning it over before cashing it. About a year later he gets his first foreign assignment.

He's in Mozambique in the back of a Toyota Hilux. He feels sort of like he used to when he'd ride the bus with Sheehan. Only now there's the jet lag and the southern light, and the realization that everything smells different.

He's sitting on top of his Pelican case in the bed of the truck. They pass a church painted fuchsia, with arches that could have only come from the Moors, via the Portuguese. They're on a road in Maputo filled with trucks and open-air markets. A freeway overpass has been closed off for all the tents and foot traffic. He can see the Indian Ocean, a green smear in the distance. It's lined by high-rises, some half finished with their skeletal walls and crane derricks.

By the afternoon, they're out of the city. It's still hot, but the wind's blowing past, and his sweat is drying. Sugarcane is burning in the fields, and the air smells charred and sweet, and the sky is snowing ashes.

He's paired with another American who's also named Robert. They've been assigned to profile a European NGO that's using rats to clear land mines. The other Robert is a writer and a teacher at some college in Georgia. He's been covering Africa on and off for maybe a decade. He's a regular contributor and pitched the story.

They've been together since JFK, and he's been saying, since at least the food court, that the magazine didn't need to spring for a second ticket. They could have used someone local or driven up a photog he knows from Durban. He has a few other freelance leads lined up after they're finished with their main assignment. They'll probably split off, he says, when they get back to the capital. For now, they've got two days in the deepest darkest, in the goddamn heat with their fucked-up dreams from the malaria medication. They probably should have stopped somewhere back in the city and grabbed Ellis a mosquito net.

"I've got one," he says.

"Hey, have you ever seen a pouch rat? They're fucking huge, but they're light enough that they don't set off the ordinance. They can smell TNT, and they're smart enough to know they get a cracker if they let the big, pink guys know about it. How's this guy walking in the middle of the goddamn road? I haven't been in the Third World in a while. It always takes a day or two to get your squint right. Don't drink anything that isn't in a bottle. Or anything from a glass with ice in it."

They find the NGO at a government clinic just before nightfall. The Belgians and their local team are set up in a linoleum-tiled storeroom that smells like wood chips and floor polish. The rats are lined along the wall in clear plastic cases. They're cleaner and closer with their handlers than Ellis expected.

He shoots a roll of black-and-white film as the woman in charge lifts one from the shavings and feeds it a banana. She's maybe forty and grew up in in a town called Ostend. She keeps smiling and saying in her accented English that she loves Africa and the work they're doing. She also keeps switching back to Dutch and whispering to the animal. The rat is the size of an Abyssinian cat and sniffs her neck, then gently takes the piece of banana she's holding in her fingers. It stands on its hind legs to eat and walks back and forth, from arm to arm, across her shoulders when its finished.

Ellis and the other Robert sleep on cots in the far wing of the empty infirmary. The room is air-conditioned by a generator and sealed off with heavy windows so they don't need their mosquito nets. They've kind of given up on small talk by this point—they don't really like each other.

When Ellis wakes up in the middle of the night, the other Robert is wearing a head lamp and reading Conrad.

"Bad dreams?" the other Robert says without looking up from the pages.

"Not like Marlow's," Ellis answers.

The team sets up a grid in a yam field in the morning, using small metal stakes and butcher string. They run a guy wire around the perimeter at roughly knee level and attach a pulley system that allows the rats, clipped into harnesses, to work a pattern across the search area. When one smells something, it marks the dirt by scratching, and the woman from Ostend calls it back with a clicker and feeds it. They clear the field, grid by grid, sending in a bomb tech to check the marked zones with a metal detector. The rats can clear twice the acreage per day than humans can with just a minesweeper.

They stop in a village on their way back to the clinic. The locals have built low rock walls along the footpaths in the unswept areas. Most of the kids in town have been told where they can and cannot chase each other. It was worse back in the '90s, they say, before they knew roughly where the resistance movement scattered most of the ordinance. Still, just last year, a woman went in after a stray cow and set off a toe popper.

Ellis finds her at the water pump in the center of the village, leaning on an aluminum crutch and yelling at her children. She knows why he's there with his camera and mostly ignores him.

He's on a hotel balcony in New Orleans the following August. He's watching the helicopters over the Superdome and the searchlights over the darkened city. He's wearing jeans and a long-sleeved flannel button-down. It's hot as hell, but the mosquitos are out, and god knows what they've picked up from the bodies in the water. He can see a McDonald's to the north with people on the roof eating cold hamburgers.

The night, with its humidity and stink of river silt and sewage, feels sort of like Africa. The floodplain, with its sunken houses and cars, has the same kind of destroyed and terrible beauty. He can't help but think about the thinness of civilization—of how the only thing separating America from some of the places he's been is a little electricity, faster internet, and more pavement.

It's nothing a storm can't wash away, he thinks. It's nothing that can't be swept from the earth by man—like the towers and that woman's leg—or like this city and his mother by an act of nature.

Part III

Flight

18

ELLIS RODE into the town of Ocaña at noon. The day had grown hot, and he wore sunglasses from his pack to cut the glare from the road. Near the center of town, he passed a row of concrete buildings spiked with rebar. In a plaza, a guard held a shotgun beside the entrance to a bank, its windows covered by metal grates.

He turned the dirt bike onto a side street and cut the engine and checked the fuel gauge, which read close to empty. Adjusting the straps on his pack, he crossed the street to a phone booth, the weight of the dog in the duffel bag warm against his ribs. He rested his forehead against the plastic walls inside and reached into his sock. He counted his money—forty thousand colónes—and watched the plaza.

When he dialed the US country code, followed by his father's cell number, a recording came on in Spanish. He tried to feed his American Express card into the slot marked *TARJETAS TELEFÓNICAS*, and it jammed in the opening. He hung up and unzipped the duffel bag to check on the puppy.

She ran one paw along her snout and began to pant, then tried to turn over in the bag. He placed his hand on her belly.

Outside, a truck hit a pothole in the street, and he flinched, then looked up, breathing quickly. As it pulled away across the side road, he slumped back against the wall.

In the plaza, a taxi stand stood between two utility poles, a man selling diced fruit in plastic bags to the drivers. Two policemen pulled up on Suzukis and began to speak with the fruit vendor.

Watching them, he stepped out of the phone booth and walked the dirt bike into an alley without starting the engine, the puppy in the duffel bag whining quietly.

•

He pumped three thousand colónes of fuel at a gas station on the outskirts of town and bought a map and a bottle of water from the attendant. The gauge on the dirt bike reset when he turned the key in the ignition—still half empty.

Drinking the water, he searched the map for the US Embassy in San Quintín and traced a wide, red line down the center of the Ocaña Peninsula, marking the only highway to the south. He connected a series of sub-roads winding in the same direction. According to the key, a car-ferry dock sat at the southern tip of the peninsula, San Quintín to the east on the far side of the Ocañan Gulf.

A man was grilling chicken in a stall across the parking lot. Ellis walked the dirt bike behind a dumpster, then paid two thousand colónes for a breast, a thigh, and another bottle of water. The cook handed him a paper bag spotted with grease, and he sat beside the bike and lifted the puppy from the duffel bag and gave her a piece of chicken.

He tore more meat with his fingers and ate, drawing his legs in behind the dumpster, watching the road that fed in from the highway. When they were finished, the puppy lay in the shade on the pavement, and he poured water into his cupped hands, and she drank quickly. Then he dried his palms on his pants, high on his thighs, away from the mud from the road, and packed the bones into the paper bag.

Blinking slowly, he pulled the puppy onto his chest and leaned back, riding the edge of sleep. He pushed his back against the wall to stand, shifting his legs, and decided to sit for another minute.

Soon he was following his mother somewhere along a freeway. She kept moving out into the lanes as the cars passed, and the air was cold, and the water beyond the overpass and the sky were the same color. He had something he wanted to say to her, but he was small, and she was too fast for him. A fish stirred in a puddle on the shoulder, sliding past his ankles.

When he woke, the water bottle was still cool against his forearm, and a man was at the pumps fueling a Datsun. The puppy had climbed down from his chest to lick the insect bites on his ankles.

He bent stiffly, lifted her, and tucked her back into the duffel bag.

Three kilometers south of Ocaña, he left the paved road to follow a dirt track that ran to the ferry on the gulf coast.

•

By the time he realized he was lost, heavy black thunderheads had begun to pile up over the mountains. Nearing the shore, the grasslands retreated into the jungle, and the ocean came into view in the west through the trees, and he shivered on the bike in the day's broken heat.

The rain began near dusk—the Pacific, wind-whipped and gray in the growing storm. He stopped to cover his pack with a rain sleeve and then drove on. The town of Socorro was no more than a cluster of buildings set down irregularly in the dripping trees. He passed pale faces in the track, Americans and Europeans. Some held magazines overhead as protection from the rain. A girl, who had straight bangs like Kara's, crossed in front of him.

In a pulperia near the beach, he paid for a beer and a packet of jerky. The beads of moisture on the can were cool compared to the rain, and he ate in his wet clothes, dripping at the counter.

When he was finished, he asked the cashier if there was anywhere to spend the night. "*Muy barato*," he said. "I don't have much money."

He skirted potholes filled with opaque water, riding back through town the same way he had entered. He found the hotel just as the storm intensified, the rain marching in lines driven by the wind, and followed a sign that read *OFICINA* into an outbuilding.

Shivering in the air conditioning, he rang the bell on the counter, then paid the clerk in cash and signed a ledger with a false name and passport number. He tucked the last of his money back into his sock and walked the bike behind the hotel, leaning it in a shadow. Above him, the main structure rose in a stand of palms, the lights already switched on in some of the windows.

He climbed the stairs to the top floor and found his room near the end of the breezeway. He bolted the door behind him and closed the curtains and then undressed in the bathroom and placed the dog in the shower. Under the nozzle, he shampooed her and washed his body. The soap ran down his legs, turning gray, mixing with the mud from the road and the dead insects from the puppy's haunches.

He dried her with a separate towel and unpacked his camera and laptop on the bed to inspect them for moisture. He patted his lenses with the edge of a pillowcase and set them on a desk near the window. Then, turning out the lights, he climbed into the bed with the puppy.

•

When he woke, he sat up immediately in the darkness. Thunder broke softly, very far in the distance. He went to the desk and turned on his laptop. When he couldn't find a wireless network, he checked along the base of the walls for an Ethernet cord but found only the phone jack. He dialed zero from the phone on the bedside table. Another recording came on in Spanish. The clock on the table read 2:16 a.m.

He dialed zero again before hanging up and going into the bathroom.

He switched on the light and splashed his face at the sink. In the mirror, the water ran down his sunburned cheeks, and he watched his eyes—ringed with dark circles. Then he cupped more water and ran it through his hair and across his forehead.

The puppy came into the bathroom and sat on his foot while he sat on the toilet. She rose when he rose, her nails clicking on the tiles, following at his ankles. She lay on a towel while he hunched over the tub to rinse his clothes of the mud and small fragments of wood that had sprayed back from the tires.

He turned out the light and placed her back onto the bed and pulled the blinds open slightly at the edge of the window, looking down into the courtyard. He positioned a chair in the corner of the room so he could sit and watch the entrance. Lightning flashed, too far away for him to hear the thunder, revealing the sheets of rain as they would have looked in daylight.

As the darkness returned, he saw his father and his mother and the truck his family had packed to move to Long Island. He remembered the shape of her behind the screen door at their house as she watched him ride his bicycle in the street. He was in the backyard, not long after his tenth birthday, when his father told him she was gone, finally.

They were feeding the birds, the sparrows picking at the sunflower seeds on the lawn. He hadn't cried until his father rested his hand on his shoulder.

"Let's go out for a while now," he said. "I'll get you something to eat. I'll get you whatever you want."

Later, when he started shooting, something in his photos made it easy for him with the girls he still knew from childhood. They seemed to think there was a part of him they could fix when they saw the restlessness in his exposures. He had even used his photos of Afghanistan, including the firefight in the poppies, though he had only been embedded for two weeks and had shot little that had run.

Now he tried to remember why he even went to Central Asia. Mostly, he decided, it was because the magazine had agreed to send him. The Afghan War also seemed to make sense on a level of cause and effect, and he felt compelled to remind people that it was still there.

Iraq had been the story then, Fallujah, Tikrit, and al-Zarqawi. Afterward, however, it became clear that his images of the Daichopan district—its scrub and scree, its mountains and insurgents, who were almost ghosts in the dark—had only served to teach him about his own fear.

He remembered waiting for something to happen in the dry, ancient light and thinking of how even boredom could be laced with death. The length of those days seemed very much like being back at his mother's bedside, watching the sun highlight the remains of her hair. The immediacy of his terror, once he saw the Marines spreading quickly through the flowers, was new to him, though, and he was overcome by its ability to drain the world's color, then amplify it in small bursts, showing him everything he would lose if he were killed.

In his mind, he saw the clay walls of the town near the poppies and the glint on something thin and silver in the cloudless sky. A building exploded, and the shock wave washed over him, vibrating the air from his lungs. The drone banked, obscured beyond the spout of dust and rubble. Then it approached again, a high point of metallic light, and fired another missile into the village.

He had repeated to himself that he was a coward as the buildings burned, and the soldiers climbed down into the valley without him. Even then he had known that statement wasn't true entirely.

Afghanistan was just the baseline he never wanted to cross again, and he had accepted other assignments afterward that were dangerous—walking before dawn on the waterfront in Durban, searching for images among the smoking shacks in the hills of São Paulo. He believed those photos were also important and were also worth the risk.

He watched the courtyard now, listening to the rain. Fear had never been something he could control with any assurance. In the poppies, it had seemed unreal until he looked at his photos. Other times, it had blinded him, like the glare of sun on ice, making it almost impossible for him to shoot.

Some men were able to control their fear, like the soldiers who climbed back into the valley. Most existed on a scale, and he wondered if man had developed this instinct to survive in the same way the jefe's dogs had been bred to ignore it.

When he had tried to explain part of what he believed to Kara, as he had understood it then, she assumed that he was only drunk and wanted to sleep with her. He also felt, almost immediately, that she understood the way he saw things and that often she viewed them more clearly.

"Hold on," she said, tapping his phone on the bar with her finger. "You're talking too fast. Just show me a few photos."

"You want another one of these?"

"I should switch to beer."

"Why would you do that?"

"Alright," she said. "Whatever. Now show me."

"Can we have two more Wild Turkeys?"

"All of your images in this stuff are moving."

"They're in focus."

"I know. They're sharp. There's just this crazy sense of motion. I can feel what it was like for you to be there. I can feel how frightened you were."

"Yeah."

"Your landscapes are nice, too. But you should stick with this. You shouldn't try to be something you're not."

His friends, by comparison, didn't seem to understand anything. They simply commuted from one fixed point to another, and because their paths had been straighter, they appeared to be ahead of him. It made him feel better to think that they were jealous of his ability to see the things they couldn't. However, in the moments when he doubted his own talent and his own choices, he wondered if he was the one who was jealous.

Mostly, all he knew for certain was that they rarely listened when he described the people he had photographed—and he felt sorry for them for working in finance, or whatever it was they did when they climbed out of Penn Station. He also judged them for their choices. They had given up on the things they'd wanted, and had been rewarded for it. Maybe some of them never wanted anything except for the money to begin with.

He never cared about how much they made, he told himself, and he truly believed this until they actually became rich and started to buy houses and have children. And the only reason he cared now was because they had looked at him—and at his apartment and his sneakers—and considered themselves to be superior. They were rich because they deserved to be.

After the agent's offer, he had imagined what it would be like to tell them about how much his photos were worth and buy them a drink in that place they all seemed to like in midtown. He knew the work itself and his retainer should have been enough, but they weren't. Then maybe he could also stop taking money from his father.

When he was younger, Ellis never thought much beyond the idea of his father on the train, riding between islands. There had never been a reason for him to question his job or the image. The trading floor and the money had always seemed to fall away whenever his father came walking across their yard.

Something changed, however, once he saw people like his father begin to manipulate the market, and as he watched his co-workers lose their jobs at the magazine, and as food and oil prices fluctuated beyond the laws of supply and demand, all the while two wars were being fought. Then in Fresno, toward the end of his drive across the country, he spotted a tent city beside an overpass.

The tarpaulins, rising and falling in the wind, housed whole families. He stopped and photographed a man who had worked in construction. He pressed his face to the camera under the nylon and trained his lens on the man's children. They stared at him without smiling in the blue light, their water pistols leaving lines in the dust. He decided then that the money that had fed him his entire life, which he spent on cameras and cabs, and on drinks with girls before and after Kara, came with a cost that his father had never considered.

We were all here at the expense of someone else, he said to himself now, thinking of the photographer he had replaced at the magazine, then of the oil jacks in Los Angeles and the cattle in Utah. Even the rancher was part of that system.

He had blood on his hands, and so did Ellis. Every time he ate or drove, he thought, he was a source of suffering. He passed it down the line. He traded it like his father with his derivatives. And he had shot that photo, and the magazine had paid him and run it and sold ads against it, and someone had found the jefe's son, and now they were going to find him and do whatever.

He went to the bathroom again and splashed his face. Then he took the map from his backpack and unfolded it. He looked out at the courtyard, where the storm continued to thrash the palms. He drew the blinds and switched on a desk lamp and ran his finger up the Pacific coast of the Ocaña Peninsula and found Socorro in the soft light. He tapped a black graphic of a plane, which sat just inland to the south.

Then he turned the map over to study an inset of San Quintín, looking across the gulf to the embassy. He measured the kilometers between the city and the hotel and compared the distance to the airstrip and thought of the needle on the bike's fuel gauge, hovering just above empty.

He slid under the sheets on the bed and, as he set his head on the pillow, pulled the puppy in beside him. She moved onto his shoulder and tucked her muzzle beneath his chin. The lamplight made her look very thin. Her nose was cold now, and she seemed softer and still smelled of soap.

After a moment, she crawled down from his shoulder and sat in the loose sheets at the foot of the mattress and nosed his foot free from the covers and began to lick the bites on his ankles. He switched off the lamp.

"Good girl," he said, closing his eyes. "Lie down."

19

THE SOUND of the door rattling woke Ellis sometime after daybreak. When he opened his eyes, the clock on the bedside table was dead, along with the electricity. He lay still as, outside the window, a shadow shifted, then stopped. He slid from beneath the covers, breathing very quickly, and moved away from the puppy.

In the courtyard a rooster crowed. He lowered himself onto the floor at the edge of the mattress and lay at the foot of the bed. The door rattled again, accompanied by the sound of the wind. Then the shadow shifted at the edge of the curtains, and he listened for footsteps in the breezeway or the vibration of footsteps on the stairs at the end of the landing.

Sliding across the floor, he moved to the edge of the window and looked out over the sill, pressing his body against the wall.

Outside, the storm had passed and the sky was clear—the breezeway empty. Torn fingers of clouds ran overhead in the rising light, driven by the wind. The palms bent and righted in the courtyard under the force of each gust, a tree on the west side of the enclosure swaying, its fronds casting a moving silhouette across the edge of his curtains.

He covered his mouth with both of his hands. He exhaled and slumped down onto the floor and looked over at the puppy on the bed.

She was resting her head between her paws and followed him with her mismatched eyes. She stood and walked to the edge of the mattress and cocked her head.

When the door rattled again, she raised her ears and barked, watching the shadow moving along the doorframe. He scanned down into the courtyard for the bike, which still stood against the outbuilding, and pulled the curtains farther back and checked the road.

"It's only the wind," he said to her.

The puppy wagged her tail and barked again, then ran in a circle and jumped from the bed.

In his lap, she licked his hands, and he pushed her away from him. She squatted submissively, looking back, and peed on the carpet. He picked her up and turned her head from side to side, holding her face up to the light at the edge of the window.

"You're going to have to stop doing that," he said. "I know you've been sick."

She pulled away from him and mouthed his fingers, then licked his forearms and sat on his foot while he peed in the bathroom. He washed his hands, and when he glanced into the mirror, he could only see his outline in the dark, even with the door propped open.

The wind continued to move the shadow of the palm across the window. He took a tube of toothpaste from his backpack and brushed his teeth with his finger and tried not to think about Kara, or the outline of her body blurred from the steam on a mirror in a hotel in Montauk, or where she might be now, or who might be with her. He saw Hull and how close he had passed in the moonlight.

"What happened to the power?" he asked the puppy.

He took a clay soap dish from a counter beside the sink and tore whatever was left of the jerky from the pulperia into small pieces and placed it into the tray. He sat on the floor at the foot of the bed as the puppy pushed her snout around his fingers and ate.

When she was finished, she crawled up onto the mattress and slept while he showered in the darkened bathroom. His clothes were still damp and heavy but now smelled of soap. The electricity came back on as he was tying his sneakers.

He paced back and forth from the window to the bathroom. His hips ached from the bike, and he was cold in the wet clothing. He repacked his bags and covered the pack with its rain sleeve and shouldered it, tightening the straps. Then he took a sheet from the bed and used it to line the duffel bag and called to the puppy.

She stood, tilting her head, and he bent to reach for her, but she skulked across the mattress with her ears laid flat. He came around to the other side of the room and caught her near the pillows and laid her into the duffel bag feetfirst, his hand cradling her chest.

She licked his wrist as he pushed her head back into the bag and zipped it. He stood quietly for nearly a minute while she pushed her body against him and sniffed through the fabric, whining quietly. Then she lay down and was still.

At the window, he watched the courtyard, and looked along the length of the breezeway and quickly descended the stairs to the office. A clerk appeared when he rang the bell—older than the man from the previous night, rumpled and exhausted.

Ellis passed him the room key.

"*Buen día,*" the clerk said, checking the ledger. "I apologize for the power."

•

When he opened the door to the internet café in Socorro, he smelled coffee, bacon, and air conditioning. An old woman appeared from the back of the space and looked at him for a moment, her skin sagging in loose folds from her neck.

She held a spray bottle in one hand and a rag in the other.

"*Lo siento,*" he said, and felt the puppy stand up in the bag. "*Lo siento. Cómo estás?*"

"*Todo está tranquilo,*" she said, and tapped her watch. "But we do not open until eight. Nothing in here is ready."

"I'm sorry to bother you," he said. "I just have to get online or use a phone."

She looked down from his face to his bags and the damp clothing that hung from his body, checked the clock, and sighed and motioned him toward the banks of pay phones and computers.

"Okay, caballero," she said.

He met her at the register and paid for a bottle of water, two glazed buns, a phone card, and twenty minutes online at one of the monitors.

"Dad," he said, and cupped his hand over the receiver as his father's line went directly to voicemail on the landline. "It's Sunday, the twenty-first. I didn't call before I left, but I'm in Nicoya and I'm in trouble. I'm going to try to charter a private plane or something to get out of the country or get to the embassy. I'm going to have to use your Amex. I'm safe for now, and I'm going to try to call the magazine after this. But I need you to call the embassy in the city and tell them what happened. Give them my name, tell them what I do, and tell them that I was here to sell some photos to a buyer named Garcia. Tell them that I flew into Iberia, and they rented me a car and that they have my passport."

An automated voice in Spanish came through the earpiece, so he hung up and dialed again.

"Check your email," he said. "Check your email as soon as you get this. I'll send you an email with everything you need to know. Call the magazine, too, if you can. Ask for my editor. His name's James Gibson. He's helped other guys get out of situations. And answer your phone. I'll call you again later."

He hung up and read the clock on the wall and tried to connect to a line at the magazine, but it was too early, he realized, even in New York—especially on a Sunday.

He moved the bags aside and logged on to a computer with a view of the street, which was still quiet. As he sat, he counted what was left of his change and ate the buns, which were sticky, breaking small pieces off from the corners for the puppy. Then he drank the water and zipped the bag.

He pulled up his email and dried his palms on the thighs of his pants and selected his father from his contacts and typed all the names and places he could recall, along with his passport number, listing the amount the jefe had wired into his account and his flight number.

He removed his camera from the pack and attached it to the monitor and uploaded an image of the jefe and Padaratz in the box at the arena and sent it as an attachment. As the email buffered, he glanced again at the woman, who was setting out cups for coffee, before he ran a search for the US State Department.

When he heard the doors behind him, he half stood, pushing the chair back suddenly as a man and woman entered, both young, in sarongs and backpacks—pale lines showing against the sunburned skin on the girl's shoulders. She was speaking French.

He sat back down and opened the website for the embassy in the capital and read the options near the bottom of the screen, searching for a phone number or an address in the city. Then he scrolled up to the center of the page, which was segmented into a local news section, and saw the jefe's bloodshot eyes in an image.

Industrialist Juaquín Janvion Decena Garcia and US Ambassador John Wells Finalize a New Deal to Co-fund Five English-Language Schools in León and Apartadó.

He reopened his email in a new window and dropped the link to the story into a message and sent it to his father, along with another photo of the jefe.

He looked up at the clock again and checked the windows and took his bags and went to the door.

"*Gracias,*" he said.

"*Por nada.*"

•

He waited in a patch of shadow in the plaza for a car to pass before he crossed into the sunlight. A dog trotted alongside him in the track toward the pulperia, then broke off, and moved to lie down with a second dog on the steps beneath the awning. It had just set itself down when both animals stood suddenly and snapped at each other, circling over a dry patch of concrete. Then they disappeared in the same direction, side by side, their reflections elongating in the puddles.

At the bike, he unzipped the duffel bag and set the puppy down and waited as she turned in a circle and squatted, a thin line of mucus trailing behind her. He lifted her once she was finished, her heart beating in his palms, the skin under her armpits smooth and hairless, and zipped her back into the bag and slung it over his shoulder.

It took him four attempts to start the dirt bike, kicking and repositioning his weight over the ignition. He flicked the needle on the fuel gauge with his finger, which rested just above the edge of the lowest marker, and engaged the transmission.

As he rolled forward into the track, a man came walking toward him, carrying a carbon fiber fishing pole, his face so tan and laced with capillaries that, in the city, and without the pole, Ellis would have assumed he was homeless. In this context, he assumed he was American.

He passed him without stopping and turned inland, then circled back and pulled alongside him.

"Do you speak English?" he asked.

"What else would I speak?"

"I was just making sure."

"I can barely hear you anyway over that piece of shit rice burner."

"Can I get gas around here?"

"You mean other than eating breakfast at the pulperia?"

"I'm just looking for a gas station anywhere outside of town," Ellis said. "Maybe a place on the way to the airstrip."

20

HULL FOLLOWED the eastern shore of the Ocañan Gulf, passing the slanted fishing towns rarely visited by tourists. He stretched his legs at a gas station outside of Tecan and spoke with the mechanic in Spanish. Howler monkeys rustled in the jungle, roaring occasionally along with the compression brakes from passing semi rigs. The man accepted a thousand colónes and took Ellis's passport and held the booklet open for a moment, shook his head, and returned it.

None of the pawnbrokers near the airport in San Quintín knew of an American selling camera equipment. In the afternoon, he met one of the jefe's men off Calle Tigre and sent him to watch the international terminal, then visited the hotels close to the embassy. He spent the rest of the day showing the desk clerks Ellis's photo, claiming he found the passport on the sidewalk near the consulate.

It had begun to rain by the time he finally settled in to watch the front gate, where a Marine guard was posted. He parked the Cherokee in a slot with good sight lines and crossed the street to a food stall and ate a *plato casado*, standing under the awning in the dark, drinking coffee, and watching the runoff.

The air in San Quintín, in the cool elevation of the mountains, felt dry and light on his skin, even with the rainfall. Someone had strung laundry between two buildings and had forgotten it in the weather.

The city was like the other Latin American capitals he had known—crooked and gray, power wires running across the alleys from glass transformers, and box fans spinning in the windows. The only difference was that this one was cleaner, even though the high-rises still thinned to shacks on the hillsides, and the streets smelled of smoke from the slums.

He stood and thought about how the rich seemed to live in the hills along the coasts and on plateaus in the mountains. It probably had something to do with positioning for disaster, he decided, man-made or otherwise.

The scent of the street, of fresh water and wet tar, made him reconsider Ellis somewhere in the storm. He was surprised the photographer had not arrived in the capital ahead of him. He also knew that anticipating the decisions of other men was unlike anything else he had ever attempted, and he had seen so many things over the years that he was unable to rationalize.

His wife had stayed for longer than he had expected, for example, even after it was clear to both of them that something had run out of him after El Salvador. There was also no explanation for why those three men in

Usulután had taken their own lives with their sidearms while the rest of their cadre waited—almost calmly with their cigarettes—to be overrun and executed.

The SAD had taught him to examine repetition for patterns, to identify what might be probable given certain conditions, then to project potential outcomes, sometimes using incomplete pieces of information. The wars, with their blurred, confusing engagements, had also led him to reject doctrine unless doctrine could be adapted specifically to a situation.

Anticipating need and reaction was often more valuable than any strategy or tactic—so the mites would be into the dogwood tree, he thought now, once the insecticide had washed away in the rain, and Ellis, on the dirt bike, most likely would have stopped due to the weather.

He crossed back to the Cherokee and watched the Marines under the lights at the post. Sometime near midnight, he caught himself dozing and reached back to open the bag that held the shotgun, and took a vial from a pouch inside, which also held compression bandages and antiseptic. He shook a Captagon into his palm, split it with his thumbnail, and swallowed half with the dregs of his coffee.

The pain in his knees fell away at some point without him even realizing its absence. He found himself sitting upright, gripping the steering wheel, riding the amphetamine. The sharpened light over the guard post seemed to outline each drop of rain slanting across it. He could hear his heartbeat and blinked and sat licking his lips, listening for a dirt bike engine.

At dawn, he checked the incoming number on his phone and looked back up at the embassy gate, the rim of the sun visible behind him.

"He just logged in to his email," the tech from Dallas said. "He accessed it from an IP address in Socorro. I just pulled it apart. He was there maybe three minutes ago. He was in and out of his email twice. I guess this guy's never heard of Tor. He sent three packets to a corporate account registered to William Robert Ellis, his father."

"Forward me the messages."

"You're not going to like what he had to say, so I took the liberty of cleaning it up. We already knew that his old man works at a firm on Wall Street, so we had an algorithm ready to penetrate their servers. It was something I borrowed. They were using two-five-six encryption, so we couldn't have handled it just using the hardware here, but I tucked this piece of source code away when I left my last job. I figured it might come in handy. I also just deleted two messages on his father's voicemail."

"Has he turned on his phone?"

"No. But he's starting to make contact. He's using landlines, which is smart. We can't exactly pinpoint his position, but if he's in Socorro, we can move on that location."

"Keep in mind that the Zetas don't stop because we have a problem."

"Understood."

"The OIF and the INL don't stop. Remember that."

"Understood."

"This still takes priority."

"We're clear on that."

"Did he make any other calls?"

"It's hard to tell. We haven't seen anything on any the other voicemails or lines we're monitoring, but I can't know for sure. If he makes a person-to-person connection from a landline to a landline, we're going to have a containment problem."

"As far as we know, that hasn't happened, correct?"

"As far as we know."

"What about the credit cards?"

"I'm not seeing anything on any of the lines of credit we're monitoring."

"Send me the coordinates of the IP address in Socorro."

"I've already done that."

"What else?"

"That's about it. We've hacked his father's cell phone and uploaded a piece of code that will power it off whenever certain numbers come in. Anything incoming with a Nicoyan country code will kick that into operation, plus the photographer's cell number. We did that with his top five cell numbers from the last three months. One of the phones wasn't on, so we couldn't access it, so we went down to number six, but, whatever, after his third contact, the frequency dropped off dramatically. Your guy is kind of a workaholic. The code was written for smartphone OS, so it won't work on landlines. There's nothing to penetrate. But all his frequent calls are to cells anyway. Other than that, we've just been trying to track him with whatever footprint we can find. And hacking the cell towers, which is complete."

"Nice work."

"Any other directives?"

"Call me if anything changes," Hull said, and hung up and dialed his men in the Prado in Cárdenas.

"*El fotógrafo está en Socorro,*" he said. "*Estuvo en el café internet al oeste del centro del pueblo hace cinco minutos. Recuerden, él está montando una moto. Pero podría haber conseguido a un coche o un camión.*"

"*Comprendo.*"

As the sun continued to rise, the glare from the whitewashed walls cut into his vision. He squinted and imagined his garden inside the compound, and the spider mites in the blossoms on the dogwood tree, and noted how the insects' legs always drew inward when he crushed them at the abdomen, in the same way that men who had been shot in the spine curled their arms and wrists from the nerve damage.

He pulled up a map of the Ocaña Peninsula on his phone and zoomed in and found nothing in the area that suggested it might be vital to the photographer.

Then he panned out slightly, and he saw an airstrip.

He redialed his men in the Prado, rolling up the Cherokee's windows.

"*Búsquelo en el aeropuerto,*" he said. "*Que se parezca a un robo. O a un accidente. Comprende?*"

"*Comprendo.*"

"*Bien. Vaya con dios.*"

"*Igualmente.*"

He switched on the air conditioning and watched his phone, waiting for it to vibrate.

•

The next valley was much hotter and drier, the puddles in the track already shrinking in the morning heat, the mud at the edges splitting into fissures. Ellis passed a plywood sign nailed to a stake with faded letters that read *Lubricantes.* The tree branches closed over him, then broke apart in alternating flickers of shadow and sunlight.

Through the thinning foliage, he spotted the edge of a painted steel girder and banked the bike up a concrete ramp into a dirt lot that had been graded and paved at its center. He parked beside an earthmover, which lay dormant, and looked over a row of gas pumps rusting without hoses. A cloud of flies buzzed in the shade of a tin roof held up by struts.

He left the bike idling as he jogged over to the kiosk at the edge of the pavement. The shack was empty—the windows unwashed, the drywall inside bare and featureless. He drove back out of the lot and passed a construction site and the skeleton of a hotel, its roof unfinished and spiked with rebar. He was about to turn back toward the fork in the track when he saw another wooden sign that also read *Lubricantes.* He entered a corridor lined by rows of tin shacks with clotheslines strung across small clearings. Rain barrels stood under the eaves, and shallow pits smoked with cook fires. He downshifted the bike as two women cradling infants watched from one of the yards.

In a field of yellowed grass and baked earth, a pack of children chased a soccer ball. Outside of the village the jungle dropped away on a hillcrest, where someone had nailed a plastic motor oil sign to a conacaste tree. He drove up the road to the top of the rise. He followed it down to a shack composed of four I beams driven into the earth. The walls between the posts were formed by chain link fencing, and a man sat in the shade under a corrugated roof, a row of steel drums lined on a network of wooden pallets behind him.

Ellis dismounted, and the attendant stood up from his seat. In the light he was much younger than he had appeared initially, his body thin in a way that suggested drug addiction or malnutrition.

"*Buenas,*" the man said. "*Gasolinas?*"

"Yes, please. *Por favor.*"

"*Cuál?*"

"*Perdón?*"

"*Qué tipo?*"

"*No entiendo.*"

"What type, bro?" the attendant asked, almost without accent. "Do you want leaded or unleaded?"

"I don't know," Ellis said. "Whatever I can get the most of."

He unfolded the last of his cash, and the attendant slipped the money into the drawstring of his shorts. Then he bent to take a closer look at the chassis.

"I can top it up for this," he said. "That bike, it likes unleaded mixed with oil."

He filled a jerry can from a spigot on one of the drums and took an empty water bottle from a box in the shack and cut off the base to create a funnel. He unscrewed the gas cap and inserted the mouth of the bottle into the opening and poured, pausing every few seconds to listen to the tank.

"Those bags look heavy, bro," he said. "This will take a few minutes."

Ellis opened the backpack and took out the rest of his water from the café and drank. He unzipped the duffel bag and placed the puppy on the ground, where she stretched her forelegs and lapped the water he poured into his hands. Then she lifted her ears, sniffing the air, and sat on the attendant's foot.

"*Hola perrita,*" he said, gesturing with his head. "It's cool. I like dogs."

He rested the jerry can on the seat of the bike and squatted to scratch the puppy.

She licked his hands, which were blackened with oil.

"Thank you, little one," he said, and she began to gnaw on his boot, fitting the side of her mouth around the edge of the sole, pressing down with her molars.

"Hey," Ellis said. "Don't do that."

"It's okay. *Como se llama?* What is her name? It is a she?" The attendant lifted the puppy and looked between her legs. "*Claro.*"

"I don't know."

"No, it is a girl."

"Yeah. I know. I mean, I don't know what her name is."

"Well, she should have a name." He set her back on the ground and poured more fuel into the bottle. "Then what is your name?"

"Robert."

"*Mucho gusto.* I am Marcelo. You don't speak Spanish?"

"Not really."

"*Un poco* but not enough?"

"Where'd you learn English?"

"My uncle owns the pulperia in Socorro. Do you know it?"

"Your English is good."

"Yes. I worked for him when I was young, and we had a lot of gringos, surfers, and tourists mostly. My uncle speaks English and he taught me and I learned some in school. But I learned in the pulperia the most. And I lived in LA for a little while, but that was after I learned English. I remember my uncle saying to me, if I can speak Spanish and I can speak English, I can speak with almost anyone in the world."

"So you don't work for your uncle anymore?"

"Now I work for me," the attendant said, and turned his attention back to the funnel. He tipped the bottle to the rim, and the fuel seeped through the rifts in the sawn plastic. "What else do you need? Something to eat? *Mota?*"

"No thanks."

"Do you want me to check the plugs and the oil?"

"I'm out of cash."

"It's cool," he said, and ducked back into the shack and returned with a rag and knelt to inspect the engine. "This machine isn't new."

"Yeah."

"What is it that you do for work?"

Ellis looked back at the road. The puppy left the attendant to come sit on his foot. He heard an engine in the distance and picked her up. The children laughed in the field while playing soccer. "I sort of work for myself, too," he said.

"That is good. I have always thought that is important, to not have to depend on anyone else. Do you have family?"

"Just my dad."

"No wife?"

"No."

"No *hijos*?"

"I guess I'm not ready."

The attendant nodded. "How old are you?"

"I'm twenty-eight. I turned twenty-eight last month."

The attendant wiped his hands and pulled the bike's dipstick and ran it through the rag, then reinserted it and pulled it back out. "Happy birthday," he said, reading the level mark. "Your plugs and oil are fine. But you are an old man for this country. I have two boys already. I am thirty and my oldest is already twelve."

"I have some friends who have kids."

"That is why I thought it was important to buy this place to work here for myself. My boys are playing soccer today. And tonight we will all go to church. But I am working now because it is important for my family to be happy. Maybe one day my boys will take this place over, or do something else for work. They are smart. But for now I want them to have fun and go to school. You will understand when you are a father."

Ellis looked out at the pack chasing the soccer ball in the sunburned field, then to the oil drums. He thought of a portrait of his father he had developed in the bathtub in his apartment. His Hasselblad had captured the sky over Long Island, thin in winter with its high striations of cloud. His father stood next to his bird feeder, his face slackened like it always was on the days when he unloaded the city from the corners of his eyes.

He tried to imagine what it must have been like for his father to be alone for such a long time and how much his father had given up by staying on the trading floor. He couldn't see himself doing that for anyone. He had never shown his father the photo.

"That's good that you have this for your kids," he said to the attendant. "I saw another gas station on my way in. Is that yours too? It wasn't finished."

The funnel feeding the bike ran dry, and the attendant poured more fuel into the bottle, cocking his head again to listen. When the liquid drained, he rattled the funnel until only a thin pink line remained near the bottom of the mouthpiece.

He pulled the bottle from the opening, and the overflow ran into the dirt.

"No," he said. "It's not mine."

He screwed the gas cap back into place and wiped the chassis with his rag. He ran his hands over the puppy's head.

Ellis let the dog slide from his arms, and she lay down in the sun and closed her eyes.

"It is not anybody's now," the attendant said. "There are a lot of things here that people start—did you see the hotel on the road? Big plans. There was a gringo developer working there, but I heard he ran out of money. And the gas station was going to be built by Petroleos de Nicoya, but they have put the project on hold. That land is for sale now."

"That's good for you."

"It can be. But I will not buy it. I own this land already. And they have put in some of the pumps and some of the lines, but they have not dug the pit for the holding tanks. Or put in the tanks yet. So what is the point?"

"You don't have the competition."

"There is another station like mine on the other side of town. But you are right. That would have been a big gas station. But I know these people and they know me."

He took his hand from the puppy and gestured over the hill toward the shacks. "I grew up here," he said. "If a big business wants to put me out of business, they can try. But these people, they know me, and I have fixed their cars and their bikes. I've fixed their outboard engines so they can fish. And I can find other work. I can fish or even work for my uncle again if I have to. And my kids are smart. They will not have to work here. Or to fish or farm."

He held up a finger. "They speak excellent English, and there are more tourists all the time. There are opportunities. Or maybe they will move to the capital and work in computers. I only want them to be happy. I want them to want to work hard. They need something for themselves, even if it will be difficult for them, because that is how they will find their own way through life when I am gone. Do you understand this?"

"Yeah," Ellis said. "My dad did the same thing for me, I think. He did a lot of things he didn't want to do so I could do the things I did."

The attendant made a face like he was speaking to a child. "If you know this, then I think you are old enough to be a father," he said. "You are an old man for down here. Now take this one, she will be good practice, even though she is sleeping again already."

He handed the puppy to Ellis. "They get so tired so fast," he said, running his finger along the bridge of her snout to the indentation between her eyes. "I wish I could sleep like that."

"She's been sick," Ellis said.

"I see."

"Do you want her? You should take her."

"My wife would kill me."

"What about your boys?"

"You know the answer to that. I tell them yes too much already. But no, you also know, if you know any women, that my wife is the one who must say yes to this, and I know she will say no."

"What's over those hills?"

"There are some farms and an airstrip. Then there is nothing."

"Is the airstrip close?"

"*Más o menos.* It is a few kilometers."

Ellis opened the duffel bag to tuck in the puppy. Her legs dangled in sleep, and the attendant stepped forward to hold the bag open.

She blinked her eyes as Ellis set her down.

"Good-bye, *perrita*," the attendant said. "It was nice to meet you."

The engine turned over the first time Ellis kicked the ignition.

He turned east, and the attendant and his shack grew smaller in his mirrors. He lost them eventually behind the grass on the hill.

21

THE JEFE sat at his table on the night of the fights with Padaratz and the girl from California. He sawed strips of *carne a la plancha* from the serving trays and stuffed them into his mouth. Sometimes the meat stuck in his throat. Whenever this happened, he would chew what was left behind faster, talking around the food. Occasionally he would pause to drink water or drain a bottle of Aguila. Then he would continue with whatever he was saying while his guests picked at their plates.

"I bet you were very happy with the main event tonight," he said to Padaratz during the second course. "My scatter bred was big, but that didn't seem to slow down your dogo, *sim* Jairo? What do you think? What do you think? I will have another dog ready for you the next time you visit, I can't even talk about it now, but bring that dogo back, I think Emilio and I will find a match for him. I can't think about it anymore. Did you see that report on CNN about the US and the Mexican border? Do they think the Zetas will just go home if they bring the federales in to help on the other side? They don't understand. *Es una situación imposible.* They trained them with their own military. They won't go away. *Ganarían más dinero si les ignoraran.* I doubt it will even help us. Let us talk about something else. How long have you been a textile buyer, *hermosa*? Did you tell me already? I bet you are very good at what you do. Have I told you about decorating this house? I was back and forth from San Quintín too many times to count. Eventually we just had to fill two Matson containers in the US and have the rest of it sent—the furniture, I mean, and some of the artwork.

It would have taken forever to find it all here. It was very expensive. I could have killed someone."

He dripped saline into his eyes during the silences, laughing to himself to fill the void. The laughter seemed foreign even to him when it came. It felt as if someone was pulling a rope somewhere, or pulling it from within him and laying it onto the table.

As he ate more meat, he slowly became aware that his eyesight had narrowed to darkness at the edges. The sensation felt, as it always did, like someone taller was standing above him with a hand over his face, close but not touching.

He fixated on four points of light, each a reflection on the tine of a fork in the serving tray. As the darkness grew around him, he watched small boils of grease shimmer in the meat drippings. He spoke faster, and the faster he spoke, and the more he ate and drank, and the more rapidly he breathed, the thicker the darkness became, until he could barely tell where he began and the wall ended.

Padaratz and the girl were on their feet as soon as he finished his dessert. He trailed them down the hallway as they walked through the house, and came to a stop between them, blocking the front door.

"I thought you were going to stay," he said. "This house, *hermosa*, it is very comfortable. In the morning we can have eggs and banana pancakes, and *gallo pinto*, and maybe watch Emilio work the dogs. He takes some of them into the fields on Saturdays, and on Sunday there is a nice service at the church in town. We will have eggs and pancakes tomorrow, how do you like them, and then we will go to church."

He picked up a phone on the wall and punched a button labeled *COCINA*. He delivered an order for their breakfast.

"I think it is better that we go, Janvion," Padaratz said.

"You should stay. Look."

"*Tienes salsa en la boca.*"

"Do I?" the jefe asked. He hung up and pulled his sleeve down over his fingers and wiped his mouth.

"*Que te sientas mejor*," Padaratz said. "I will see you soon. I promise." He kissed his friend on each cheek.

Upstairs in his room, the jefe watched the Range Rover's headlights wind down the hill, his fingers fidgeting with the bottle of solution in his pocket. After what seemed like a very long time, the wall of darkness began to thin and his eyesight widened. The hand over his face withdrew, but when he lay down, it returned and the shadow thickened.

He closed his eyes, wrapped in Egyptian cotton. He watched faces form and dissipate in the darkness like drops of ink in deep water. Breathing faster, he thought of his son and of himself as a boy, his father holding the wire of a coat hanger. A puddle of urine spread across the dirt floor of their house in León as the metal cut across his back. His scatter-bred mongrel drew in a breath in the pits below the arena. He saw his son again, then the photographer, and then the photographer's portraits.

He rubbed his face with the back of his wrist, his eyelids burning. He stood up, trying to back away from the darkness over his face, and sat in a chair at the foot of the bed. The floor seemed to slide away from under the Persian carpet. Then he was no longer in his bedroom.

He paced the halls in the dark and found the bathroom and opened a bottle of pills.

"Take these," the American doctor had said at the boarding school. His breath smelled metallic and old, like he had eaten fish for dinner. "You're like your father. You know that I know him?"

"No."

"Well I do. Do you take other medication?"

"I have allergies."

"What kind?"

"Hay fever."

"Well, that's fine, son. I've never told your father this, but he's a little moody. We can fix things like this now. Calm down. We're going to fix you right up. I want you to take one of these when you need to relax."

The jefe returned to his chair to watch the moon, which was still lost behind the wall of darkness. He closed his eyes and turned into a street in León he didn't recognize from his childhood. The shacks around him, which seemed to close in on him, made him realize he was dreaming.

It was still early, the sky underlined by a thin band of red, when he woke in the chair. He descended into the foyer, his feet silent on the polished marble. The windows in his office were still layered with condensation, and he shivered when he entered.

He applied his eye drops at his desk, then shook the mouse to wake the computer. He opened Ellis's external hard drive and clicked through the portraits from Los Angeles. The photos of his son brought the hand back over his face, the shadow resisting the pills.

He opened and closed folders at random, leaning forward from time to time to inspect the images. He lingered over a self-portrait that Ellis had shot in the rearview mirror of a car. A road ran straight behind him into the desert. In the distance, something seemed to be pooling across the highway that looked like water or ice—the lake of a mirage.

The office walls shifted from gray to pale shades of orange. He lay down on the carpet in one of the beams of light and rested his head on the floor. The scent of butter cooking drifted in, and he smelled eggs and coffee and something sweet, like vanilla and burned sugar. He almost had fallen back asleep when he heard footsteps in the hallway. He rolled over, turning toward two dark shapes at the base of the door.

"*Dónde están sus huéspedes?*" the maid asked. She carried the banana pancakes and eggs on a tray into the office and set them on the desk. "*Desayuno para tres,*" she said.

The jefe sat up and tried to remember her name. A different woman came and took the plates away, then delivered flautas for lunch under a metal lid. Eventually she brought the meal back to the kitchen uneaten.

He spent the evening as he had spent the day—on a couch on the far side of the study while an American news network broadcast mutely on the flat-screen. He applied his drops and swallowed the pills from his pajama pockets. He silenced his cell phone each time it rang.

Rubbing his eyes, he got up from the couch and went to the empty kitchen. He ate a cold piece of chicken, standing in the light of the open refrigerator. He wiped his hands on the cuffs of his sleeve and went to the window to look across the compound at Hull's outbuilding. Still chewing the food, he shuffled upstairs to his room, where found the hand and the presence waiting for him.

The rainfall outside was muted by the tempered glass in the windows. He tried to sit in the chair again, this time with his mind cleared, breathing slowly. The harder he tried to keep his thoughts at bay, the less control he seemed to have over them when they came. He saw his son at seven years old.

"*Los edificios son muy altos,*" the boy said.

"Speak English when you are in Los Estados."

"I said the buildings are tall."

"I know what you said."

"Well, they are."

"I know this. What else do you think?"

"It's loud."

"Louder than León, yes?"

"So much louder."

"What else?"

"The people," the boy answered.

"Yes. The people. They are faster."

"And there are more of them."

The jefe laughed—nothing like his laughter at the dinner table. "You are right," he said. "There are more of them. But it takes a certain breed of man to live in a place like this, James. Do you understand this?"

"No."

"Well, what do you see?"

"I see them rushing."

"They are moving toward the things that they want. You would be rushing, too. Only men with ambition can survive here and make the things we have seen. What did you think of the statue?"

"She was green."

"And what else?"

"She was tall."

"You are right. She was tall and one hundred and six years old. And she is not American. But she is here and she is a survivor. Like me. Like us. Are you hungry?"

"*Un poco.*"

As they ate, the jefe had imagined the boy becoming a man, time dripping away as fast as the orange grease on their pizza. Now in the bedroom, he revisited this future and saw that it could not have been, that it would not be. He thought of his son's execution and then of his dogs—of animals that were of no use despite their potential, and of others that would fight and win despite their scattered breeding.

In each case, he knew that their bloodline only played a part. The handler and the trainer were given material, both good and bad, and asked to mold it. The result depended on their methods.

The woman from the kitchen called to ask him what he wanted for breakfast.

"*Nada,*" he said, and ordered a cheeseburger.

He ate the beef without tasting it, followed by the pills, watching the muted news as the wall gradually began to thin around him. He dozed upright in the chair.

A heat began to build behind his eyes, forcing the hand and the darkness away from him. He applied his drops, beating the edge of the desk in a light rhythm with his fist.

On the veranda, birds were drinking and flitting in the puddles. Leaning against the window, he looked down at the driveway to the sleek, black Range Rover and the photographer's rental car beside it.

He went to his desk and took the hard drive and dropped it in the trash, then dialed Hull's cell phone.

"He's in Socorro," the American said. "The team in the Prado should be on-site already."

"And where are you?" he asked.

"I'm waiting to see if he gets past them."

Part IV

Butterflies

and

Vultures

The man on the passenger's side of the Prado looked over at the driver. He laid the Kalashnikov on the back seat and covered it with a beach blanket. He thought of his wife, her hair blowing on the shore as she bent to collect shells. He rolled down the window.

"Amigo," *he said.* "Con permiso."

He made a motion with his head toward the gas shack attendant, who walked from the shade of the roof toward the truck.

"Buenas," *the attendant said.*

"Qué onda?"

"Nada. Y tu?"

"Nada. Has visto a un yanqui? Perdió su pasaporte y nosotros lo tenemos. Es un amigo nuestro. Viaja por moto."

The attendant leaned inside the truck. "No," *he said.*

The man on the passenger's side pulled a bill from his pocket and rested it on the doorframe.

"No?"

The attendant shook his head.

He unfolded two more bills, and the attendant looked behind him toward a row of shacks and a soccer field hidden behind the hill.

"No. No sé. Ya te lo dije."

"Está bien."

He counted out seventy-five thousand colónes and peered into the back seat as if he was looking for something before moving the blanket to reveal the stock of his rifle.

"Un norteamericano," *he said.* "Es nuestro amigo."

He pushed the money out so that the tips of the bills touched the front of the attendant's shirt. "Un yanqui."

The attendant looked toward the soccer field again.

"Él estaba apenas aquí."

"Fijate," *the man on the passenger's side said, and allowed the money to fall to the ground.* "Qué bueno. Hace cuánto estuvo aquí?"

"Más o menos diez minutos. Dijo que iba a la pista."

The driver unfolded a map. The attendant leaned farther into the truck to trace a route with his finger.

"Está aqui," *he said, and tapped the icon of a plane.*

22

THERE WERE cows on the runway, long-eared and lank, thin Brahman cattle that walked with a grace lost among the denser breeds in Utah. Ellis shut off the bike and glassed the herd with his 200mm.

The animals were strung out in a line across the airstrip, folds of loose flesh sagging from their necks, their hooves leaving dimpled prints on the soft tarmac. An egret landed between the lead bull's shoulders. The bull held himself very still as the bird picked for insects along an ear. Then he shook his head, and the whole herd began to move off the runway, lowering their mouths into the grass beyond the pavement.

Ellis swept his lens up the valley toward the terminal, a simple concrete frame, painted yellow. In the heat, the building wavered. The crescent of a river lay between the runway and the jungle. He scanned for men at the edges of the fields, panning to the dark wall of trees in the distance. He looked across the river's banks to the yellowed grass in the valley.

Nothing moved other than convection lines and the cattle. He dismounted the bike and walked out onto the track. When he looked back through the viewfinder, he saw a wingtip just behind the terminal. He took another step and brought the plane into focus. A parrot lifted from the crown of a palm at the end of the runway. He watched as another bird joined it in a flicker of red.

He remained still, studying the gravel parking lot next to the terminal. Another parrot appeared, followed by a flock of smaller birds, which fanned out across the hillside. Below him, their shadows flitted over a field of boulders.

He was on his way back to the bike when he thought he heard an engine. At first, the sound was so faint that it was almost lost in the breeze, and he stood with his legs set apart, holding his breath as a gust of wind blew across the hilltop, puffing up earth and skittering gravel. In the stillness afterward, he heard it clearly—a whine of acceleration.

He pulled the duffel bag under his arm and scrambled from the track up an embankment. He weaved through a stand of brush that pulled at his clothing, the dry wind filling his mouth with the taste of the earth.

Kneeling to the ground, he aimed his lens back toward the valley, where in the distance a plume of dust spiraled into the heat, enlarged by the 200mm. At the base of the vortex, a Prado raced across the flatlands, weaving back and forth on the track.

He stumbled down the bank, knocking dry earth and dead twigs into the road. He mounted the dirt bike as the puppy thrashed against his ribs.

The engine seemed close now.

"Lie down," he screamed, and opened the bag and stuffed the camera in beside the puppy. Then he set his foot on the ignition and pushed her head back into the opening and zipped her in and started the engine.

The Prado crested the hill just as he accelerated into the track, and he watched the truck for a moment in the rearview mirror—huge in the reflection. He pinned the engine, and the hill rolled away in a blur of earth and cattle, the Prado pulling even with him, the muzzle of a pistol appearing in the driver's side window.

Something flashed and snapped past his head.

He flinched, hitting the brakes, and the bike fishtailed, the duffel bag whipping across his chest, causing the puppy's weight to jerk his shoulders.

The Prado roared past, and he turned the handlebars away from it and released the brakes as the truck cut broadside, skidding in a fantail of rocks and red brake lights.

Another flash exploded from the window.

The sound ripped through the air beside his ear—and the truck left the road, sailing through a line of saplings, throwing bits of shattered wood before coming down in the field of boulders.

He accelerated into the dust plume, which was drifting across the track, and the sunlight faded into a deep tunnel. For an instant, all he could see were the handlebars in front of him and the ruts in the road. Then it was as if he was watching the bike pass through the cloud from outside of himself. It moved in and out of view, like the drone above the poppies, and he saw the showered earth from the missile strike and the shimmer of a fuselage in the sky.

When he emerged into the sunlight, he blinked the dust from his eyes and shifted into neutral and opened the clutch. In the relative quiet between gears, the sound of the truck came from somewhere below him. He stood up on the pegs and found the Prado still running downhill, through the scrub, bouncing on its tires through the gaps in the boulders.

When he lost sight of the vehicle, he was left with only the air rushing past him and the hollow, rubber hum of the studded tires. The puppy was standing now against his ribs, jerking frantically.

"Fucking lie down," he screamed.

He pinned the throttle across a straightaway at the base of the hill, and the airstrip flickered past him. Turning his head, he searched again for the plane but could no longer find it. He banked around a bull, which was yoked by a wooden board across its shoulders.

As the track bent away from the terminal, he entered a stand of trees, and the air grew cool. Suddenly the bike skimmed over a rise, and in the green light, the river cut across the road ahead of him, where cows were sunk up to their knees in a wallow.

He was already speeding across a gravel spit, halfway into the river, before he found the brakes with his fingers, sheets of water fanning up, obscuring his vision. The cattle appeared through an opening in the torrent, their tongues lolling over squared teeth, their gums blackened at the edges. Then the front tire of the bike grazed a boulder and tore the handlebars away from him, and he leaned back, abandoning the seat, and grasped for the steering column.

The chassis twisted violently between his legs and was gone. He watched the bike climb the far bank without him, wheeling on its back tire. He floated behind the wreck, over the surface of the river, and slid, legs first, through the water—the gravel along the bank running up his pants, tearing through his palms and into his ribs.

His sneakers caught in the mud, and he flipped onto his chest, his face dragging into the gravel. It was very quiet once he came to a stop.

He became aware of the leaves rustling and watched a shadow. The sky fell backwards, folding into a patch of gray light in his vision.

He reached for the straps on the duffel bag to untangle them. He could feel something in his palms. His legs were still in the river. Some instinct gave him the need to clean his face, and he tried to use his right hand to brush something from his cheek, but his fingers would not open.

He drew a breath, and a bright arc of pain shot across his ribs, followed by a clicking sensation under his skin, in his bones. He felt his vision lift away from him as hooves passed alongside his head. He leaned over to vomit, and a stream of water dribbled from his lips and nostrils, billowing away into the current, flecked with blood and white specks from his chipped molars.

The pain flashed across his ribs again, and he almost slid back into the river. He had lost one of his sneakers, he realized. He heard the Prado somewhere behind him. The birds, which had settled back into the trees, took off again as the sound grew louder.

He crawled up from the waterline, then limped onto the track, where he found the bike, its engine still running. Holding his side, he righted the chassis and swung his leg over the seat and pushed off with his toes, engaging the transmission, which caused the bike to surge forward.

The tires crabbed in the soft earth, out of control, and he weaved drunkenly toward the jungle. A tree branch whipped across his body and thumped hollowly on the duffel bag, then bent back as he released the throttle. He touched the ground with his feet, almost blind from the pain in his ribs, and spit and glanced over his shoulder.

The Prado crested the hillock on the far bank, a thick cloud of smoke rising from its grill. The truck was close enough now that he could see the men inside through its smashed windshield. He feathered the gas, and the bike shot away from the trees.

In his broken mirror, the truck descended into the stream and raced behind the bank. He heard the rush of water, followed by the impact of something metallic, and a cow staggered up from the river, dragging its hind legs, trailing the blue rope of an intestine.

He looked forward to where the trees thinned, and the light shifted and flared, suddenly blinding him. He felt little pain now and stretched his body as close as it would lie to the handlebars.

The Prado emerged from the trees, jumping across the cracks in the reflection, rocking in the track, the muzzle of a machine gun flickering in the window.

A fence post exploded beside him.

The bike seemed to glide over the tiny ridges in the dirt as he accelerated. For an instant, he thought he saw a strip of flame rising from beneath the Prado's hood, then the doors opening and a silhouette aiming a rifle alongside the burning engine. By the time he took his eyes from the road to look into the mirror, however, the truck was already gone, bleeding into the horizon.

·

Hull lowered his head to listen.

"Calm down," he said. "*Calma. Despacio por favor*. How big is the brush fire?"

"*Es grande.*"

"Is the vehicle operational?"

"No."

"Destroy the VIN numbers and license plates," he said. "And get away from the accident."

He called the jefe's cell phone, which went to voicemail, then dialed the landline for the hacienda.

One of the women picked up in the kitchen.

"*Dónde esá el jefe?*" he asked.

"*El jefe está durmiendo.*"

"Wake him up."

"No. He hasn't sleep for two days."

"I talked to him an hour ago."

"Now he sleeps."

"I need to speak with him."

"I cannot. You know what happens with him."

"Which driver is on today?"

"*Qué?*"

"*Cuál conductor trabaja hoy?*"

"Carlo."

"Put him on the phone, please. *Quiero hablar con él.*"

The mouthpiece clattered, and the line went still except for the occasional whisper of a knife being sharpened in the background. He switched his cell phone to speaker and plotted a course from the embassy to the ferry docks in Punta Prieta. Then the phone clicked, and someone picked up a separate receiver.

"*Habla Carlo,*" the driver said.

"Where's the jefe?"

"He no goes outside for two days."

"I want you to take the Range Rover to Socorro."

"*Yo no puedo*. I can't go with the Range Rover without *el jefe*. Unless he say."

"*Conoces a los hombres en el camión, los tipos en el Prado? Los hombres que he enviado a perseguir al fotógrafo cuando lo perdimos en el estadio?*"

"*Sí.*"

"You have to pick them up outside of Socorro."

"*Sí?* But *el jefe?*"

"They had an accident. *La policia*, and the OIF. They are going to be looking for them. The oil pan, you understand *la palabra*? Oil pan?"

"*Sí.*"

"They tore the oil pan out of the truck."

"*Mierda.*"

"It started a fire. You need to pick them up before the *policia* find them. Before the *policia* call the OIF. *Comprende?*"

"*Chingado.*"

"Tell one of the women I told you to take the Range Rover. And tell them to tell the jefe to call me as soon as he wakes up."

"*Sí.*"

"Check in when you get there. I should be on the twelve o'clock boat to Cartago."

"*Cartago? De Punta Prieta?*"

"*Claro*," Hull said, and started the engine.

23

ELLIS LOOKED up through the bare trees at the skeleton of a radar tower.

The air smelled of snow.

"What did you say?" he asked.

"I said, I thi—here—time of ye—"

"Kara, I can't hear you. You have to turn to face me. And stop talking into the wind."

She lowered her Leica, her eyes framed by her hair. "I said, I like Montauk, especially at this time of year." She turned back to the reeds, and a shutter clicked. "What are the names of these things again?"

"I can't remember," he said. "Wait. They're called phragmites. That's what my mother used to call them."

"Phragmites. They're beautiful."

"Let me see your shots," he said, and she held out her camera.

He handed her his Canon as the sun passed behind a bank of clouds, shifting the sky to gray.

"You think it'll snow?" she asked.

"This one's nice," he said.

In her photo, the seedlings blew from the tips of the stalks, twisting against the orange backlight behind the swales. He could see the same objects laid out in front of them but not in the same way. She had done something with the composition and the light that he couldn't follow. The same clouds were in the sky, and the same brush was in the foreground, but she had seen the darkness coming before it was even there. The image was incredible.

"You know what I was thinking?" she said.

"What's that?"

"This is going to sound weird."

"Okay."

"I was thinking that it might be cool to do a project where, after people die?"

"Yeah?"

"You'd go and take photos of the things they loved. Or the things they'd just touched, or used, or something. Like, if someone had always drank from the same cup, and people could see that, with their lipstick still on it, or whatever, they could see it was one of the last things their grandmother had touched, maybe that would help them. Maybe it would help them remember her. You know?"

Now she was shooting with his camera. "Maybe it would help them decide," she said. "What to keep and what to get rid of. I don't know."

"That *is* weird."

"Shut up."

She smiled as he slid his arm around her waist.

"No, it's interesting," he said. "I never thought of something like that. It's a little morbid. But you should see if you can make it part of something bigger. Maybe like something that's about the objects that are associated with each stage of life."

"Maybe."

He kissed her, but she pushed him back.

"Wait," she said. "What's this thing set on?"

"The light's gone," he said.

"No, it isn't."

She looked down at the main dial and adjusted the f-stop on his Canon, along with the speed of the aperture. The phragmites rustled in the wind.

"Where should we go for dinner?" he asked.

"Hold on."

He saw the blink of the shutter.

"We have to get back to the city," she said.

"What time?"

"My flight's at eleven fifty."

"JFK?"

"Yeah."

"So should we eat out here?"

She looked at her watch. "Are you hungry?"

"Yeah," he said, and they exchanged cameras as they walked.

"I'll call Harvest when we get back to the hotel," she said.

"You're excited."

"This is a big assignment."

"It's just an assignment."

"You'd take it."

"Everyone we know would take it."

He switched his settings to monochrome near the edge of the woods before they reached her car. He shot a sink that had been thrown into the brush. The rust from its faucets had stained the porcelain basin almost black.

"Now who's being morbid," she said.

"I'm going to miss you."

She looked out at the ocean. "Things are just moving fast for me now."

"How long will you be in Morocco?"

"I don't know," she said. "As long as it takes, probably." She took a breath and held it, then lowered her camera.

24

HULL ROCKED the Cherokee over a speed bump and dropped the truck into neutral. He rolled to a stop beside a church and waited, tapping the gearshift as a cluster of children filed through the chapel doors and crossed the road. Their uniforms—the sky-blue shirts, their trousers and skirts of light-gray cotton—looked impossibly clean and pressed, somehow free of sweat.

At the edge of town, he checked the map on his phone and accelerated down toward the coast. Thin patches of gray distortion, like small pieces of fog, were laced between the power cables along the highway. He leaned forward to look up at them and realized they were massive spider webs strung between the lines.

He checked the speedometer and shifted his legs. He squinted in order to read the kilometer markers beside the road, calculating the distance to the ferry. He mapped another route in case the photographer reached the mainland before he could cut him off on the peninsula.

They had another eight to ten hours, maximum, he decided, until they would lose control of the situation. He still had his lockbox in the capital, he thought, with the clean passport and cash—he could be out of the country in three hours if his position broke down with the jefe.

Then he would be back where he started before he left Virginia. He'd planned for unimaginable scenarios all of his life, but he had not expected to be released on disability or to lose everything in his 401(k) in the recession, and he hadn't planned for the splinters of metal in his legs or on getting married so young, only to have them both consumed by his deployments, and the silences between them.

At first she had enough energy to get anything she wanted, he thought. Eventually all she wanted was to preserve whatever energy she had left. She tried to keep them both moving forward, together, each time he came home. He tried digging in their yard in the spring and building fires for her in the woodstove.

On long rotations, they would have good stretches, when he could sit with his back to the tree line. However, he was always eventually pulled into the explosion on the waterfront or caught by some other memory that bled into his mind. At some point, the fact that she couldn't help him, and the rigidity of his withdrawal, offset everything else.

She was in a bar without air conditioning in Fayetteville, wearing cutoff jeans and talking to another officer. He could see a birthmark high on the back of her thigh. He sat down with both of them, almost by accident, and then it was just the two of them at the jukebox.

"What are we going to play?" she asked.

"I don't know much about music."

"That's a lot of dimes for someone who doesn't know how to spend them."

"That's why I need your help."

"And you wanted to get me way over here. Away from him."

"I hadn't thought of that," he said, and she laughed and clacked through the vinyl.

"We did country growing up," she said. "And my granddaddy was an architect, so he liked Beethoven. He also went in for Vivaldi. I remember those violins in the house."

"Did they live with you?"

"They owned the land. We had a place at the other end of the field, but there was always something on the stove over there, my grandmother cooking something, or growing something, or cooking something she'd grown. So my two sisters and my little brother and I were usually in their kitchen. Or with her in her garden, looking for handouts."

"We're not going to find Vivaldi in this place."

"I wouldn't think so."

"One of my grandfathers liked Mahler," he said. "I remember that. But he was from my mother's side, and we didn't see him much."

"What about your daddy?"

"The only noise he ever liked in the house was Cronkite."

"My daddy liked Hank Williams."

"I know enough Hank to know I like him."

"All you boys can get behind Hank," she said.

"What'd he do? Your father?"

"He was a sheriff's deputy. My mother's a teacher at the community college."

"You seem like you read a lot. Or like you're from a family that reads a lot."

"I'm not going to even address that."

"Did you go away somewhere after high school?"

"I went to NYU. Now I'm getting my master's from Fayetteville State at night. You know it?"

"Not really."

"I wouldn't either if I wasn't from here."

"Why'd you come back?" he said, and she looked up at his shaved head.

"Why'd you join?" she asked.

"My father was in. So was my uncle. So was almost every man in my family, going back to whenever they came over."

"From where?"

"England mostly. And some German."

"I suppose that explains the Mahler. We're Scots-Irish. And part Cheraw, according my grandfather."

"I always assumed my father wanted me to do what he did. Then I came back from the recruiter's, and all he said was to take every test and to ace them so they'd make me an officer. And that I didn't have to prove shit to him or to my uncle. And to remember that, no matter where they sent me."

"How's that going for you?"

"I've always been good at taking tests."

"I'm studying to be a social worker, since you asked."

"I should have asked. You just make me nervous."

She took a sip of his drink, which he'd set on the jukebox.

"What's that mean, then?" he said. "Being a social worker?"

"I help underprivileged families," she said. "We find them jobs. We get them into school. We help with housing. Things like that."

"Underprivileged?"

"Financially. Socially. Mostly colored."

"Right."

"Don't start. Trust me."

"I didn't say anything."

"I know what you're thinking."

"All I'm thinking is it sounds like what I do."

"Sure it does."

"I help people too."

"You're at Bragg."

"Yes ma'am."

"So you teach people how to kill other people."

"Some places don't operate under the finer points of civilization."

"That worked out well for the Montagnards."

"You can give a man a fish, right? Or you can teach him."

"We're teaching them in my line."

"I didn't say you weren't. All I'm trying to say is usually my guy already knows how to fish. And I'm helping him deal with the guy who's trying to take the fish away from him. Or the guy who's telling him he can't fish, period."

"That sounds polite. I can't decide if you're an idealist."

"Or what?"

"Or something else."

"It's a different set of rules, but it's not that different. I'm still leveling the playing field. The first step is realizing you can't shovel shit against the tide."

She punched in the code for Hank Williams and tugged once on his sleeve. She smelled like shampoo and bourbon. She had shifted her weight so her hip was very close to his leg.

"Fair enough," she said, and he brushed the birthmark with his fingers.

25

WHEN ELLIS sat up, he could not remember lying down next to the bike. He looked over to the shape of the duffel bag, which was still strapped to his body, then down at the throbbing bulge of his broken hand. He smelled smoke in the distance. Above him, the leaves shifted in the breeze, and his eyelids fluttered in the patchy light.

He leaned back, but the shift of bone in his side made him bolt upright. Holding his hand to his chest, he pushed himself up with the inside of his other wrist and leaned on his elbow and rolled over onto his stomach.

He listened to the jungle and the road for an engine, watching the light again, under the trees, and the sky between the leaves. A lizard stood motionless in the shadows, each scale outlined in orange tinting, like segments of rust. It flicked its tongue, drew itself up and down on its legs, and disappeared into the brush.

He crawled to a tree to pull himself up the trunk. The bark on the sapling peeled away and slid beneath his fingernails in thin splinters. He panted, on his knees, and continued to claw with one hand as light streaked against his eyelids. Then he tucked his elbow against his ribs and stood up.

The weight on the straps sent the pain into his chest. He pushed aside the duffel bag and lifted his shirt and reached down to touch his ribs. The skin was already swollen and blue and still packed with mud.

He breathed as shallowly as possible and picked away some of the gravel.

Nothing moved in the bag along his hip.

He readjusted the strap again, lifting it around the pain. He rested his hand on the shape of the puppy within the fabric. Then he raised his arm, carefully pulling the sling over his head, and wiped his eyes and laid the duffel bag on the ground.

In Afghanistan there had been a woman living in a cave. He rode with a UN convoy from Kabul to shoot her portrait alongside another photographer. The Spaniard already had visited her twice, and like Ellis, within the chaos of his photos, he seemed to be in a constant state of fear. She had been squatting in Bamiyan province in the ruins of two ancient statues of the Buddha. The Taliban had shelled the carvings with antiaircraft guns, then mined and dynamited them. The destruction of the site—fifteen hundred years old and cut directly into the mountainside by monks—had taken weeks.

When Ellis arrived, little remained of the statues. He climbed from the truck and crossed to the deep alcoves where they had once stood hundreds of feet high, and found a giant fingertip in the rock on the floor of the cliff face, a segment of folded robe elsewhere in the rubble. The woman, with her children and her goats, had wandered across the high desert to squat in a network of caves just beyond the Buddhas. Their walls were covered with paintings from travelers who had walked the Silk Road, the colors darkened over the centuries by smoke and handprint oils.

According to the Afghan translator, there were no religious motives behind this woman's presence. She was neither Buddhist nor Islamic. Protest against the Taliban was as foreign to her as the technology that had destroyed the statues, and the jets and helicopters that allowed the Americans, in turn, to destroy the Taliban. She simply had nowhere else to live, and the plainness of this was what had brought the Spanish journalist back for her photo.

Her indifference, he said, was so stark and human that—when juxtaposed against the destruction of the statues—it represented nearly everything about the nature of not only this war but war itself, layers of subtlety he wanted to capture in a single photo. What Ellis saw in her seemed to be even more primal.

When he was finished behind his own lens, the woman's eyes told him that her indifference was not created by war. She was only starving, and against the backdrop of her and her children's survival, the destruction of the rock was meaningless. The destruction of anything other than herself and her children was meaningless. She did not care about anything if it did not relate to her ability to draw milk from her goats and for her children to survive through the next day and the week that followed.

When Ellis opened the duffel bag, something passed across him that was like the faded paint in the caves. He saw the mask of the woman's face and her goats scrambling over the fingertip of the Buddha.

He covered his mouth.

The puppy was dead. She had bled from her ears and her nose. Her blue eye was open. She looked very small and somehow still frightened.

He slid his good hand into the bag to touch her but reached around her instead to unsnap the lockpins on his 200mm. He separated the lens, which was cracked and wet with river water, from the camera.

He took off his backpack and laid the lens inside and tilted the body of the Canon. Water drained through the mount. He blotted the sensor with the bottom corner of his shirt. He ejected the memory card and sealed it in a plastic bag with his spare flash.

He took a roll of duct tape from the bottom of the backpack and splinted one broken finger against the other. He tried not to look into the blue eye as he tore the tape into strips with his teeth. Slowly, he lifted the backpack onto his shoulders.

He wrapped the puppy in the sheet from the hotel, careful to only touch her through the cotton. He set her down in the underbrush and zipped the bag.

He took the strap, threading it back through itself, and slipped the loop over his head and tightened it around his ribs, then limped to the bike and started the engine.

In an unpaved lot five kilometers to the south, he found a *mercado*. He took two bottles of water from the shelves, a blister packet of aspirin, a pair of flip-flops, and a black T-shirt with an eagle silk-screened across its shoulders. He limped past a man stocking a freezer and a clerk reading a magazine and left through the service door behind the meat counter.

He washed the abrasions on his face in a gas station across the road. The bathroom was cluttered with oilcans, and the soap burned like fire. Afterward, he used the duct tape to tighten the sling around his ribs. He pulled on the shirt, took off his wet socks, and stepped into the flip-flops.

He switched on the light, and the walls seemed to float around him. The glass in the mirror was clouded, black and irregular at its edges. He unpacked the map, waiting for the vertigo to pass, then took the pills.

He traced a route southeast that followed a ferry line to the mainland, to the far side of the gulf into a town called Punta Prieta. He tapped the black icon of a plane just inland from the port and refolded the map.

When he got back on the bike, the ruts in the track spread the pain into his lungs and his chest. At a juncture near El Viejo, three palms stood in a cluster, their crowns stripped of fronds. A vulture sat at the tip of one of the headless stalks, fanning its wings, its feathers rippling like fingers. He passed under the bird and turned to cut across the ranchlands that stretched eastward toward the Ocañan Gulf.

•

They were burning trash in the street in Punta Prieta. Hull drove into the smoke, leaving the container ships and derricks of the industrial port at Sulaco. He turned off the highway into a road filled with traffic.

He glanced at the clock on the dashboard, then along the line of cars and across the rows of dead palm trees and teal block buildings, which funneled into a thin splinter of land to the docks.

A pickup truck approached from the opposite lane with a rack of bull-horns mounted on the cab. He rolled down his window to listen to the voice coming from the speakers.

"Paz y progreso! Ramirez por gobernador! Paz y progreso! Vengan a la reunión esta noche en el estadio de fútbol para escuchar al candidato."

The voice faded, replaced by the engines of motorbikes and the whine of an electric sander. He turned into an alley to bypass the traffic. A dog with three legs came through a doorway and chased the truck, barking at the tires. He read the election posters nailed to the telephone poles.

The alley ran into a dead end, and he reversed the truck back to an opening between two buildings. He pulled over and checked the map on his phone. The main street, which ran the length of the small peninsula, was the only approach to the docks, he saw, the only path through the shanties and the cinder block warehouses overgrown by a breed of switch grass that he recognized from Virginia.

He nosed the Cherokee back onto the main road as a boy shot in front of him on a bicycle. Mangroves lay across a narrow waterway to the north. He waited, watching the cars creep past, until a man in a delivery truck waved him into the lane. He dried his neck with the sleeve of his shirt and thought of the cold earth under his dogwood trees. A boatyard beside the road smelled of dead fish and fiberglass resin.

The soccer stadium, very much like the jefe's arena, with its high cement walls and ring of seats, scrolled past on his left. He passed the main gate, then a security checkpoint manned by three OIF on dirt bikes. A scaffolding and stage were being erected on the field.

The gulf came into view, a milky color, the inshore water lightened by the shallow sand bottom. A jetty stretched out from the edge of the marina beyond a chain link fence. A complex of pools sat behind the wire, each drained of water, the basins littered with fronds from the palms hanging above them.

He reached for his phone and dialed zero. The operator connected him to the ferry service in Colón instead of Punta Prieta. Men with shovels leaned over a garbage pile and threw ashes into the water. The brake lights lit up in a column in the street ahead of him.

According to his map, the ferry dock was three blocks away. It had taken him more than an hour to cover that same distance in La Libertad, dragging his smoking legs through the rubble.

26

YELLOW BUTTERFLIES drifted across the track, the insects shifting in neon clouds above the sunburned blades of grass. The landscape seemed to fade around their wingtips, the leaves of the trees not green but gray, the sky pale and distant.

Ellis could no longer feel his broken hand. The only pain in his body now seemed to be the pain in his ribs. He crossed the ranchlands, growing cold, then feverish, then cold again. He hunched forward, applying the throttle in small bursts, his right arm pressed to his side where the bones grated and clicked beneath the skin.

He watched the flashes of color around him, the butterflies carrying him forty kilometers until the track began to swim in his vision.

He stopped the bike near La Secca, at the top of a small hill. He leaned on the handlebars and wiped a coat of dust from the gauges. In the mirror, his face and the bike were each covered in the same earthen film. Blood had clotted along his cheek, and rills had run back from the corners of his eyes through the patina. He spit, and the wind carried the froth through the mass of hovering insects.

A vehicle approached in the haze, a tractor-trailer hauling cattle. He sat motionless, too exhausted to move as the truck passed, its radiator layered with bits of color, the confetti of wingtips rippling under the grill.

He continued down the road, blinking away the dust. The afternoon sun drew shadows from the conacaste trees, which rose at the edges of the fields along the coastline.

By the time he drove into Cartago, the gulf shimmering in the light, he was speaking quietly with Kara.

"I can't come with you," he said.

"I might be gone for as long as we've known each other."

"So half a year. We're barely in the same place to begin with."

"We can change that."

"No, we can't."

"You can freelance."

"I can't piggyback your assignment."

"What's the difference?"

"I have stuff going with my magazine too. I just can't do it."

"Fuck," she had said. "You're such a boy."

When he looked up, there were people in the road beside him—stray dogs resting in the shade, pangas pulled from the waterline, men folding nets on the beach.

He parked the bike near the wharf, where the packed dirt had softened to sand under the tires. He stood for a long time and watched the faces of the men in the ferry terminal, a corrugated shack on pilings over the water.

In the shade of the ticketing office, he could see the movement of the gulf between the boards in the floor. The girl behind the counter looked up from her magazine.

"*Está bien, señor?*" she said.

"*Sí.*"

"You are very dirty. And bleeding a little. Would you like to sit down?"

"What time is the next boat?"

"It is okay, sir. Please sit down."

"I can't."

"*Qué pasó?*"

His eyes went down to the water and across to the men sitting along the wall. "Nothing," he said.

"*Quiere un medico?*"

"No."

"Would you like something to drink?"

"Please, I just need a ticket."

She leaned forward to study his face under the dust.

"*Por supuesto,*" she said. "*Lo que quiera.*"

She turned to her computer with its worn keyboard. Her lips moved soundlessly as she typed.

Her teeth were irregular and beautiful in a way that was rarely seen anymore in America. "Will you pay in colónes or dollars?"

"How did you know I'm from the States?"

"*No sé,*" she said, shaking her head. "I can just tell. Are you sure you would not like to sit down or have something to drink?"

"I'm okay. I'm just dirty."

"You are hurt, I think."

"I'll see someone in Punta Prieta. I just fell off my bike."

"Señor, the next boat isn't for an hour."

"I can wait. One way, *por favor.*"

"You are sure?"

"Yes."

"It is not a problem."

"I'm sure."

She made a sound with her lips and shrugged. "*Conduce?*" she asked.

"What's that?"

She closed her eyes. "Are you bringing a car, sir?" she asked. "*Un coche?*"

"*Un moto,*" he said.

"That's right. You said that."

"How much is the ticket?"

She checked a price chart beside the register. "*Veinte mil,*" she said.

"How much?"

"With the bike, *es* twenty thousand colónes."

A door opened and closed in a back room somewhere in the terminal, and he turned to look behind him. "Is there another way across?" he asked.

"There's the ferry at Pequera."

"I don't have any cash."

"We can take your card."

"Is there an airstrip in Punta Prieta?"

"*Sí*," she said. "Is east of town, but yes. Only it is faster to fly to Los Estados from San Quintín. The airport is close to Punta Prieta."

Watching her teeth made it difficult for him to think.

He wanted to close his eyes and fall under the pain, where it was cooler and much darker. He reached along his ribs for the duffel bag and was surprised to find it was missing. He looked over at the computer and followed the wires running from the register into the wall and imagined them reaching across a network into his bank in New York and transmitting back to the terminal. He saw the jefe and Hull, their faces as imprecise as his mother's in his memory.

When he gave her his father's American Express card, she swiped it, and a receipt curled from the register.

"Sign here, please," she said.

He reached for the pen with his broken hand, stopped, then took it with the other and scratched something like his signature.

She gestured with her head toward the dock. "*El barco llegará en una hora.* Okay?"

"One hour," he said.

"*Perfecto.*"

The water was bright in the window behind her. He walked to a pulperia across from the terminal and followed the dirt road back toward a sign that read *BANCO CENTRAL DE NICOYA*. The doors to the building were locked when he tried them. He leaned against the window to look inside the office.

"It's Sunday," he said to himself, and walked around the corner.

Behind the bank, he found a tinted glass door that led to a kiosk. A uniformed guard with a shotgun sat in a folding chair beside it. The man stood when Ellis approached, pointing the barrel away from him, out toward the water.

"ATM?" Ellis asked, backing up slightly.

The guard nodded and unlocked the door and watched Ellis limp up the alley. He locked the bolt once Ellis was inside the kiosk, where a cash machine was mounted to the wall, its brackets shedding flakes of paint and rust.

Ellis held his arm over his ribs and looked into the camera on the machine. Then he withdrew the maximum amount allowed from his father's card, five hundred dollars converted into colónes. He split the cash, tucking one-half into his pocket and the other into the backpack. He knocked on the door for the guard to unlock it.

Moving along the fence in the alley, he swung the pack around to his chest, careful to keep it from resting against his ribs. He unzipped the main compartment and stopped under a tree that had grown in a striated diamond pattern through the fencing. In the largest pocket, he found his cell phone beside his battery charger along with a deck of cards. He slipped the bag back on, adjusted the straps, and continued down the alley.

At a corner near the terminal, he leaned against a wall and watched the people on the dock and in the road. He turned on his phone and dialed his father's line, which rang once before going to voicemail. The sun had started to fall behind the jungle, casting beams through the trees, the light still reflecting blindingly over the water.

The wind had died, and it was suddenly hot again.

In the window of the ticket office, the fans stopped spinning. Someone on the dock cursed and yanked on a starter cord.

"*Vamos, bebe. Come mierda. Te odio. Te amo.*"

A generator shuddered to life.

The ferry came shimmering along the horizon, ghosting through the heat over the water. The men on the beach had finished packing the net and were now passing fish up in buckets to the pulperia. A driver in one of the trucks lining the dock started his engine. A flock of pelicans flew in low offshore, skimming the surface with their wings.

Kara picked up after the third ring. Her voice was soft and she sounded tired.

•

Hull tucked the phone between his shoulder and ear, and then the connection died behind a hillside. He had to wait until the freeway climbed higher before he could redial.

"You need to turn around," the one from Houston said. "I know you just missed the last boat in Punta Prieta, but get back there."

"Be more specific."

"He came online in Cartago. He's using his father's credit card and his cell phone. We deleted another voicemail to his father, but it looks like he made a direct connection on the next call. It was to a sat phone registered to an editorial account for *National Geographic* in North Africa. It doesn't look like he's ever called it before. There's nothing we can do about that right now, whatever he said, I mean, he's told someone something at this point. He also powered down again or destroyed his phone when he was finished. He knew he was blown from the cards, so he figured why not. But listen. He just bought a ferry ticket—Cartago to Punta Prieta. So you should turn around. You don't need to take the boat across from Colón."

"When does it get in?"

"Nineteen thirty. Do you still want to contain him?"

Hull turned the Cherokee around at the edge of a palm oil planta-tion. The perfect rows of trees deepened to darkness, forming a tunnel of columns that ran across the plain into the mountains. The air smelled like coconuts in the fading light. The scent filtered through the vents on the dashboard.

The tires spun in the mud before they caught and swung the truck back onto the pavement. He accelerated north on the Pan-American Highway, climbing the hill he had just passed, only twenty kilometers to Punta Prieta.

27

ELLIS LAY on the ferry deck between a crate of eggs and a cooler filled with ice and fish and dreamt of a general store with slat shingles and cows in a field, a white line of wind turbines across the backdrop. He checked for something in the road behind him. Then the light shifted, and he was watching the Prado pass through the cattle in the river.

He sat up, hugging himself to still the clicking in his ribs. He took the backpack and climbed the stairs to the deck and shuffled to a seat along the railing. The Ocaña Peninsula stretched away in the west against the black sky and the black water. The other passengers seemed to be asleep or sitting with their eyes closed, rocking with the motion of the ferry. He closed his eyes, too, then opened them again.

He thought of how late and dark it felt, and how much later it must have been for Kara in Morocco. He pictured sitting with her on the couch in her apartment, their arms touching, and imagined what it would be like to extend that moment for years. He saw the blue eye of the dog as he looked up at the unfamiliar stars over the water.

Near the opposite rail, a man in a canvas jacket sat smoking a cigarette. He turned away when he saw that Ellis was shivering. The wind blowing back over the bow smelled of burned plastic. The lights near the far shore were closer, a pair of navigation buoys blinking in the channel.

Ellis opened the backpack and held the map behind the seats to keep it from tearing in the breeze. He checked how far inland the airstrip was from the harbor. The duct tape had begun to peel away from his ribs, and he reached into his shirt to gently press the binding with his fingers. He coughed from the pain and held himself very still until his vision cleared. He thought of the bike in the hold and tried to imagine climbing back onto it. He reached into his pocket.

Steadying his weight against the movement of the boat, he crossed the deck.

"*Por favor*," he said, and offered the key for the dirt bike to the man with the cigarette. "*Quiero comprar su chaqueta.*"

•

Hull parked the Cherokee near the empty pools, away from the street-lights. He sat for a while in the air-conditioned cab and closed his eyes. Through the glass, he could hear the rally in the soccer stadium. He ran his hands together and down over his knees and turned off the engine.

Vendors with carts were strung along the waterfront, selling muli-tas and skewered meat. Couples held hands on the path that ran past the jetties. He watched the pulse of heat lightning, like the flicker of artillery, in the sky and reached into the back seat and opened the bag behind him. He took off his shirt and fastened the straps of the Kevlar vest under his armpits. He redressed and loaded the shotgun, the hollow click of the oiled receiver cutting through the loudspeaker from the stadium.

In the distance, a fishing boat rocked on the water. He drew the Sig Sauer from his ankle holster and pushed the slide back, just enough to check that a round lay in the chamber. He scanned for the ferry, then read his watch. The inside of the Cherokee was hot without the air conditioning. He slid the shotgun back into the duffel bag, which he left unzipped, then slung the strap over his shoulder and stepped out into the dark, where the sound of the rally grew sharper.

The garbage fires were extinguished, but underneath the scents of the gulf and the cooked meat and charcoal, something plastic and rotten still hung over the waterfront.

A family passed him as he walked to the docks.

"*Vamos*," he heard the father say to the two boys trailing behind him.

They ran a few steps to catch up, pulling plastic planes on a string, the toys clattering over the uneven paving.

Inside the next flash of heat lightning, their shadows passed over his feet. Then they were gone, lost against the black bulk of the jetty. He pressed his back along a palm tree, watching for the ferry. The dead fronds rustled in the pools behind him.

For a moment, the smell of meat and burned plastic and the faces of the two boys sent him back, across the Río Torola into the Morazán highlands. The air was cool where they'd touched down, and he let it settle into his skin, which was still radiating the heat from the lowlands. He stood on the helicopter skid as the wind from the blades beat the tree branches, blowing up dead needles from the floor of the pine forest.

He stepped off the skid and ran to a deadfall. Claros followed and they waited, sighting down their weapons as the thump of the rotors faded over the ridgeline—the Salvadoran Army shelling in the distance.

They began to climb, and the smell of the burning village reached them before they could even see the fires through the trees. A mist moved with the wind, thickening as they followed a path through the boulders.

They hiked for an hour, climbing upward until they came to a field of red earth and plots of sorghum.

"Captain," Claros whispered, signaling ahead with two fingers.

Hull listened, then moved behind a rock pile and surveyed the square ahead of them in the village. A sewing machine and a bicycle sat in an empty fountain. The rest of the plaza was lined with trash and broken furniture, the paving stones glowing orange from the burning houses.

Hull held up his hand when he saw a shadow move beyond the square, and Claros slipped to the other side of the pathway. Then something cracked in one of the fires, and a beam collapsed in one of the buildings.

In the burning quiet afterward, a bell tinkled and a can rattled across the stones. He signaled to Claros and pointed toward both of his eyes, then out at the square in the direction of the bell.

The receiver on Claros's rifle shook as he shifted into a firing position.

Near the west side of the plaza, three goats walked through the smoke and the firelight. The sound of the bell grew clearer and drowned out the hiss of the burning houses. The goats came across the square, followed by the rest of the herd, and passed slowly between their positions.

They continued into the forest, picking over stray bits of trash among the pines.

A boy, hardly taller than the goats, was walking beside them, his face and clothing covered in soot. He led a buckling by a rope and was wearing huaraches. He had bled a little onto his shirt from his elbow. Hull made a small chattering motion with his fingers to Claros.

"*Niño,*" the Salvadoran whispered.

The boy looked around for the voice, and when he found their painted faces, black under the trees, a dark stain spread down one of his pant legs.

Hull slid forward from the rock pile, and the buckling jerked against the rope, and the boy dropped the lead, and the goat ran back into the plaza.

In the dark, the child's eyes were invisible, even in the firelight.

"Ask him what happened," Hull whispered.

"*Qué pasó?*" Claros asked, inspecting the boy's shirt. "*Niño, qué pasó aquí?*"

"*Qué pasó?*" Hull asked softly. "FMNL?"

Claros snapped his fingers and the boy's eyes glowed orange. He looked past them to the place where his goats had gone into the forest. He pointed to the patch on Claros's shoulder, a death's-head split by a lightning bolt. Then he pulled his sleeve out of Claros's hand and followed the sound of the bell.

They found the rest of the children in a ditch behind the buildings. A vulture lifted off when they crept into the clearing. It circled, then perched on the corner of a roof above them. Most of the bodies lay smoldering in a freshly dug pit. Some sat high on the edges of the shoveled earth, their gray eyes sightless.

They smelled of burned fat and fuel and plastic. The shell casings on the ground caught the light from the remnant of the fire.

"M16," Hull said, turning a cartridge over in his fingers. He inhaled through his mouth to avoid smelling the smoke from the bodies.

"Where did the helicopter go down?" Claros asked. "With the other *capitán* from Los Estados?

"About five clicks up that ravine, according to the beacon."

"First Company reported resistance here, but there are no emplacements or RPGs," Claros said. "*Dios nos salve.*"

Hull pointed with his muzzle toward the sorghum fields.

"They're farmers," he said. "This happened before the bird went down. *Es una táctica de tierra quemada.*"

They exited the pass in the next valley at first light, watching the forest for movement, easing the soles of their boots down and stepping along the sides of their feet across the carpet of fir needles. Hull stopped in cover to wait for Claros on an incline, then stalked forward again, slowing his pace to keep the distance consistent between them. They followed a thin line of smoke curling into the pink dawn ahead of them.

They drank the rest of their water and watched the breaks in the trees at the edge of a rockfall. The smell of smoke was still on their clothing. They moved again toward the wreckage, faster in the advancing sunlight, leapfrogging through cover in the forest.

The pines gradually thickened until they arrived at the crash site. They found the helicopter hanging in the canopy, nearly touching the earth, its metallic skin showing through the scars in the paint. A rent ran back toward the tail, a scorched hollow near the rear gearbox. The blades were spread around the aircraft like a halo.

Hull came alongside the fuselage and looked into the cockpit through the shattered windscreen. A roof plate had drawn the pilot's head back. The copilot was also dead, and fire had run across the starboard half of the control panel, burning the dials.

The crew chief and the door gunner were in the main cabin against the portside firing station. Greenview was strapped into a jump seat near the rear bulkhead, in khaki pants and a blue shirt without an insignia. A line of blood had run from his fingertips and pooled, like candle wax, where the door met the floor plates.

"I can't get in there with my weapon," Hull said. "Watch our perimeter. *Un momento.*"

He unclipped his sling, set down his gun, and hauled himself into the helicopter.

The boughs sagged under his weight, and the doorframe was still warm from the fire. He braced himself against the seat that held Greenview's body, and wormed forward.

The briefcase was in an ammunition crate near the bulkhead, tucked alongside Greenview's seabag. He tugged it out of the canister. It slipped from his fingers and fell between the doorframe and the mount for the .50-caliber.

He had to hang nearly upside down, very close to Greenview's slack shoulders in the harness, to grasp it again by its handle.

"Captain Hull," Claros said.

"Contact?"

"*Nada.*"

"One minute."

He slid feetfirst out of the cabin, dragging the package behind him, and dropped to the ground. Safety glass tinkled and fell from the cockpit in fragments to land, shining among the pine needles.

He pulled a pair of wire cutters from his webbing and clipped the lead on the mouth of the briefcase. Then he snipped through a tag stamped with the seal of an eagle.

The packet inside was clean, the pages crisp and white, and he wiped his hands on the front of his shirt and flipped through them.

ATLÁCATL BATTALION AFTER ACTION REPORT / OPERA-CION RESCATE / U.S. EMBASSY, SAN SALVADOR. ON 010 DEC CPTN HULL WAS INSERTED BY HELICOPTER INTO AO VICINITY ATTACHED BY S.A.D. TO ATLACATL BATTALION UNDER THE COMMAND OF LT. COLONEL CACERES. THE CPTN REPORTED CIVILIANS PRESENT IN EL MOZOTE PRIOR TO NIGHTFALL. THE CPTN ALSO CITED A LACK OF DEFENSIVE POSITIONS.

ALTHOUGH IT IS NOT POSSIBLE TO PROVE OR DISPROVE AN EXCESS OF VIOLENCE AGAINST THE CIVILIAN POPULA-TION BY GOVERNMENT TROOPS, AN INVESTIGATION WOULD LIKELY SHOW THE GUERRILLA FORCES (E.R.P.), WHICH ESTABLISHED DEFENSIVE POSITIONS IN THAT AREA OF THE MORAZÁN PRIOR TO OPERACION RESCATE, HAD PULLED BACK ACROSS THE HONDURAN BORDER AS EARLY AS 08 DEC.

WHILE NO EVIDENCE FOUND BY THIS OFFICE CONFIRMED THAT GOVERNMENT FORCES SYSTEMATICALLY MASSA-

CRED CIVILIANS IN THE AO, IT IS CLEAR THAT GOVERN-MENT FORCES, SPECIFICALLY ATLACATL BATTALION UNDER THE COMMAND OF LT. COLONEL CACERES, DID NOTHING TO REMOVE THEM FROM THE PATH OF BATTLE, WHICH THEY WERE AWARE WAS COMING AND HAD PREPARED FOR. IT IS ALSO CLEAR THAT CIVILIAN CASUALTIES DID OCCUR DURING THE OPERATION. WHILE SEVERAL INTERNATIONAL NGO REPORTS HAVE ALREADY ESTIMATED CIVILIAN CASUALTIES AROUND 1000 DEAD, NONE WOUNDED, THIS OFFICE BELIEVES THE NUMBERS COULD BE MUCH HIGHER. WE ALSO BELIEVE THIS COURSE OF ACTION TO BE ONGOING IN OTHER AREAS OF THE AO. WE ARE STILL PURSUING QUESTIONING AS TO WHICH ARMY UNITS AND U.S. ADVISERS WERE PRESENT, AND INVES-TIGATING WHETHER THIS COURSE OF ACTION IS ONGOING.

IN LIGHT OF THIS CONFLICT'S THREAT TO U.S. NATIONAL SECURITY, THE ADMINISTRATION'S SUPPORT FOR THE CURRENT REGIME, AND GIVEN THAT AMERICAN SPEC OPS ADVISERS WERE MOST LIKELY PRESENT FOR THE <u>ENTIRETY</u> OF OPERACION RESCATE, WE SUGGEST DISTANCING PERSON-NEL CURRENTLY IN COUNTRY FROM THE OPERATION. ALL SPEC OPS STAFF HAVE BEEN ADVISED: THE DETAILS OF THIS OPERATION ARE TO REMAIN CLASSIFIED. CPTN GREEN-VIEW HAS BEEN DISPATCHED WITH THIS DOCUMENT FOR EMBASSY ATTACHÉ APPROVAL AND/OR SUGGESTION FOR FURTHER COURSE OF ACTION. CPTN HULL REMAINS IN THE FIELD ATTACHED TO ATLÁCATL BATTALION. END SUMMARY.

He took a lighter from his pocket and held the flame to the edge of the packet. They had placed demolition charges near the door gun's ammu-nition belts and along the gas tank, hiked out of the ravine, and called for extraction.

Now Hull heard a boat engine on the waterfront, the synched rise and fall of pistons. He moved in under the palms, closer to the empty pools, and bent each knee, one after the other. When the ferry docked, a Suzuki crossed over from the hold with the rest of the traffic. The bike was covered in dust and was being driven by a man in a clean T-shirt.

28

ELLIS CAME ashore onto a cobblestone path along the water and found himself in the partial darkness, filing with the rest of the passengers from the boat onto the peninsula. A series of diving blocks stood beyond a fence in a grove of dead palm trees. He held his weight up on the mesh with his good hand, shivering in the canvas jacket, and watched the cars crossing over the gangway, a line of rusting Nissans and Toyotas. A Daihatsu flatbed emerged from the hold, hauling lumber. Then he heard the engine of the dirt bike.

Someone on a bullhorn was speaking excitedly in Spanish in the street. He continued past the jetty and a cart vendor, blinking away the smoke, and turned into a crowd at the foot of a stadium. Streams of people flowed around him, entering and exiting through the main gateway. He could see a field of thin grass under the lights—the dirt pale as sand between the blades, a stage made of scaffolding.

A pickup truck sat on the sidewalk, broadcasting an announcement.

A placard, featuring a photo of a man in a suit, was taped to its doors, and the driver was passing out pamphlets.

He limped under an awning strung with lightbulbs, then along a row of storefronts filled with cell phones. He turned off the main avenue at the next intersection and passed under a leaking water tower, the drops falling across his shoulders.

He cupped his hands and washed the dust from his face. The water echoed onto the concrete and burned and tasted like the mud in the river. He held his ribs in the alley and leaned on a wall between two buildings. The windows in the shacks were dark here and stapled over with chicken wire.

He picked across a patch of broken glass, careful of his feet in the flip-flops. In the glare that shone in from the road, a shadow advanced, and he turned and saw something moving quickly in the dark, past the water tower, a shape carrying a duffel bag against its hip, limping slightly.

He ran into the darkness ahead of him.

•

Hull craned forward from his neck, his knees cracking as the photographer staggered around the corner of a building. Panting in the next alley, he lost sight of Ellis and stopped to listen for the scuff of gravel or the rustle of fabric.

He could hear him somewhere in the dark coughing. He drew the Sig Sauer from his ankle holster and watched the next pool of moonlight.

A blurred shape crossed his sights, and he pulled the trigger, and the bullet clapped into a cinder block wall, just over the photographer's shoulder.

A dog began barking nearby. He could no longer feel the pain in his legs. He fired two more rounds as Ellis disappeared around the edge of a warehouse. He turned back toward the main avenue and cut through a courtyard filled with shipping pallets.

He found the photographer in the next alley facing a wire fence—the light from the street casting his torso in silhouette. He raised his weapon, then looked past the photographer into the avenue, where people were crossing.

"Fuck," he said, and tucked the pistol into his waistband and pressed his forearm against the grip.

By the time he reached the fence, Ellis was already over it, scrambling into the street. Hull pulled the mesh back, where it was loose at one corner, and squeezed against the side of a building, sliding into the gap, cutting his palms on the wire.

On the sidewalk, he readjusted his Sig Sauer and pulled the bag with the shotgun through the opening. The crowd thinned as he followed Ellis inland, away from the stadium. The avenue split into an intersection—a park surrounded by walls of brightly painted cobblestones, sitting in the space between the streets.

The headlights from an oncoming car blinded him for a moment.

A shape hobbled into the grass and crossed into the far lane. He stepped forward as more traffic flickered past. Then the photographer turned to look back at him.

He was still wearing the backpack and the clothes from the arena. His face was streaked with mud, and he still looked very young, and one of his arms was tucked into a clean, white jacket.

Hull stepped forward and felt something catch in his knees. The headlights fell away, and the photographer became only a shape again.

•

Ellis ran along the edge of the road into traffic—a car speeding past him in a blur of light. He crossed a set of train tracks into a maze of shacks and climbed another fence and came down in a driveway lined by cement walls topped with broken glass.

A bird flapped its wings in the dark. He pressed his elbow against the pressure in his lungs and breathed with the sharp arc of pain and spit a thin string of blood. He climbed onto a pigeon coop at the end of the driveway and reached over the glass and pulled himself up onto the roof of a shack.

One of the flip-flops slid from his foot and fell away into a narrow yard filled with trash. He lay on the overhang, the metal flexing beneath him, and kicked the other thong from his foot, grazing his ankles on the glass.

When he stood up, the fence at the end of the alley rattled behind him. The pigeons beat their wings in the box. Something flashed and whistled past his head, and the gunshot echoed through the driveway.

Another muzzle flash flared below him. He scrambled forward, his knees and hands pounding the tin. His arm collapsed, jerked aside by something hot, and he slid across the metal incline, a warmth spreading down his elbow into his ribs.

He tasted blood in his mouth and inhaled, and the pain fell away, and he was on his feet again. At the edge of the roof, he jumped across to the next shack. The tiers of a construction site rose on the far side of the alley—a naked outline of girders and rebar. He scanned down onto the unfinished floors of the building.

A lamp came on suddenly in the window at his feet, followed by foot-steps on the sheet metal behind him. He turned and looked back as Hull ran to the peak of the roof and reached into the bag slung over his shoul-der. Then he jumped, and a cloud of buckshot tore into the building across the alley.

As he fell, the backpack lifted, weightless, from his shoulders— a thin stream of water reflecting the moonlight, very far away on the ground, a plastic bag rippling with the current. He passed under a beam into the building, and his legs buckled, and he slid in the dust and rolled across the concrete floor, dragging himself into the shadows.

He unclipped the backpack and thrashed the straps from his shoulders. His fingers were wet now from the blood spreading down his elbow. He crawled to his feet and limped toward a cement mixer. Through the building's open frame, he could see a warehouse rising in a sheer wall across the next alley.

He found a ladder fastened to an I beam that led upward through the ceiling. A mangrove came into view as he climbed.

He pulled his body onto the top floor of the construction site and lay flat on his chest, leaning over to look back down the shaft as the rungs swayed below him, clicking metallically. He crossed the floor and looked over at the warehouse, where a low wall ran around the flat tar paper roof, almost level with his knees. In the distance he could see the gulf again and the lights of the soccer stadium.

He took a step back and jumped just as Hull came up through the floor on the ladder. He cleared the protecting wall and fell onto his stomach, and his elbows came away black from the tar paper. He scurried around an aluminum vent and pressed his back to a fan grate. Hull fired the shotgun again, the pellets ripping into the metal.

Ellis pulled his legs in as the vent shook with another load of buckshot, and stared at the cuts from the glass on his ankles, the small ribbons of blood welling within them. Behind him, he heard the slap of boots and the skid of gravel, followed by the muted slap of flesh on stone.

When he peered around the vent, he saw Hull's pale irises, his gray face hovering at the edge of the retaining wall.

The old man tried to pull himself up onto the roof, his arms hooked over the rim of the warehouse. He still held the shotgun in one hand but quickly dropped it and raked the ledge with his fingers.

He glanced up, blinking, then looked away. A thin noise came from the back of his throat as he slid and fell into the alley.

•

Hull smelled cordite, the scent rising from his hands. He saw the firefight in La Libertad and the bats spreading across the sky. He watched the moose with his wife and fed the woodstove and smelled the pines and the river.

Then he was climbing through the forest in the highlands, breathing the smoke through his mouth. He dropped the shotgun onto the roof and looked down between his ruined knees into the alley.

As the ground rose to meet him, he smelled the soil of his garden and his dogwood trees in Virginia.

Coda

●

THE JEFE woke on the couch under the windowpanes, which were wet. He stood and stared down into the driveway at the Range Rover, where his men moved back and forth in the headlights.

Someone knocked on the door on the other side of his office, and he tied the sash of his bathrobe and went to his desk and took his pistol out of the drawer. He shut off the muted news station on the television and checked to make sure there was no one outside on the balcony. Then he opened the door only enough to see the edge of his driver's face in the hallway.

"*Qué es esto, Carlo?*" he asked.

"*Los técnicos de Hull llamaron. El OIF encontró el cuerpo de un Americano en Punta Prieta.*"

"*El fotógrafo?*"

"*No. Es Hull, yo pienso.*"

"*Muerto?*"

"*Dijeron que el fotógrafo lo mató.*"

"*No me digas.*"

He smiled and took the eye drops out of his pocket.

Kneeling, he pulled a cord in the floor and opened a safe under the carpet. He slid a bag of American cash across to the driver and set another bundle of money on the leather chair. He fired three shots into his computer and took the photographer's hard drive out of the trash basket and tucked it into his bathrobe.

"*Vamonos,*" he said. "*Espera, déjame vestirme.*"

In the Range Rover, he called the captain at the local police station and explained where to find the money. Once they reached the arena, Emilio helped him carry a new litter of puppies up from the pits and load them into the vehicle. They opened the gates to the rest of the kennels and drove them up through the side door at the mouth of the tunnel.

The jefe turned in his seat and watched the animals sniff the air at the edge of the jungle, their muzzles red in the brake lights. Then they began filing into the trees, and the Range Rover sped out the valley, moving east toward the far coast of the country.

●

ELLIS CRAWLED across the tar paper roof to a catwalk on the other side of the warehouse and leaned on the rail, unsure of how to swing his legs over the retaining wall. He was cold again and kept reaching up to the collar of the jacket to close it. His arm seemed wet with the stream running from his elbow. The jacket fell open around his ribs.

It took him a very long time to first push his good side over the retaining wall, then to drag his legs onto the catwalk. He lay on the scaffolding as the blood from his arm ran through the grates, dripping into the loading yard. Heat lightning flashed again over the water. He hooked his good arm onto the railing.

At the bottom of the catwalk, he limped around the warehouse to look into the alley. In the half-light, he watched something move, and for a moment, he thought Hull might be somehow trying to rise to his feet, then realized it was only an animal standing over the other American, drinking from the dark puddle ringed around his body.

The dog was very thin and small and kept licking its lips and furtively checking back over its shoulder, as if it was being hunted by something. When it looked up at Ellis, its eyes caught the light from a sodium lamp and flickered a grayish white, glowing without pupils.

He turned and crossed a gravel lot and paused to watch the railway. In the distance, he heard a siren.

On the other side of the factories, he came to the beach and the water. The town was dark there. He sat down. The sand was cold without the sun.

When he opened his eyes again, the tide was in around his ankles. He stood up and walked to the edge of the road, where a Prado passed, a group of children staring through the tailgate.

Another vehicle pulled onto the shoulder.

"*Necesita ayuda?*" the driver asked. "*A dónde vas?*"

"*El aeropuerto,*" he said.

"*Está herido.*"

"I need to go home."

"*Usted necesita un médico. Estás sangrando.*"

"*Aeropuerto.*"

"*En San Quintín?*"

"No," he said, "*aquí.*"

The driver nodded and unlocked the passenger's door and reached out for him.

•

The hospital in Panama sat on an old plantation, a colonial mansion in a circle of bright grass surrounded by flags. His mouth was dry when he woke.

Ellis waited for two days in the medical wing of the embassy for his paperwork to clear, eating pills and ice cream. He watched the Marines outside his window and slept.

The men in his room wore suits and had very short haircuts. Their questions made it seem like they were less interested in the jefe than the other American. They showed him a photo of Hull's body and a portrait of the same man in uniform from when he was much younger.

"How did this happen, Robert?"

"I'm not sure," he answered.

"We understand you're exhausted."

"I sent my father a photo of the man he was working for."

"Janvion Garcia?"

"Yeah."

"His property was empty when the OIF raided it yesterday."

"Let's start again," another man said from across the room. "What was the name of the art dealer who contacted you in Chelsea?"

•

He carried the puppy home from the window of a kill shelter, cutting across Houston Street with the direction of the wind, turning uptown, holding her inside of his jacket.

She slept in a patch of winter light near the radiator.

"You're going to get us kicked out," Kara said.

"She'll be good."

"She's adorable."

"They were going to kill her if no one adopted her."

"Our lease says no pets."

"Whatever."

He turned on the television and watched the survivors of an earthquake in Port-au-Prince picking through the streets, drinking from puddles, their skin chalked from the dust of broken concrete.

On the next channel he saw a photo of blood on the deck of a boat, the oiled water inside of the marina, where the authorities were unloading a body. A graphic on-screen reported the details of an incident surrounding the suspected leader of a Central American cell of the Cartel del Golfo, who was murdered near León in Nicoya. Witnesses suggested he was killed in an exchange of gunfire while fishing offshore in the Caribbean.

Several months prior, he had been accused of the kidnapping and attempted murder of an American photojournalist.

•

They took the train in the spring to Long Island, the power lines running and dipping beside the tracks. Kara left for the beach with her camera while he sat with his father and the dog in the backyard, feeding the crows and the sparrows.

"She's leaving on an assignment next week," Ellis said.

"She has to work."

"I know."

"How's work going for you?"

"It's slow."

"How're your ribs?"

"Sit," he said to the dog, and she ran from the deck and scattered the birds at the feeder.

"I saw a hawk the other day," his father said.

"Yeah?"

"I wish you were here. We have ospreys now, too, in the marsh. The town built them a tower."

"For the nest?"

"Remember when you were twenty-two, you went to the Galápagos?"

"I remember."

"They were tagging cormorants. I was proud of you."

"I know."

"I'm still proud of you."

"For what?"

"For everything."

"You shouldn't be."

"You can't say things like that."

"That was one of my first trips for the magazine," he said after a moment. "They assigned an underwater photographer, too, but they had me do the portraits and the lifestyle. They ended up using all my stuff and almost none of his."

"I didn't know that," his father said.

"I remember coming up this hill when we were on our way from the airport," he said, and tore a slice of bread into pieces. "This is something I think about sometimes. We were loaded into a van with all this gear, and there weren't enough seats for all of us, so I was sitting on the floor, and we were coming up a hill, and the driver passed this car, and in the oncoming lane, there was this dump truck. I could see it coming at us through the windshield from where I was sitting between the seats on my Pelican case. Everybody could see it. And all we could do was sit there and watch, and instead of slowing down, the driver speeds up. And the van was so slow, and the truck just kept getting bigger, and then the driver got around the car—I don't know how—and cut back into our lane, and I remember the whole van rocked from the air as the truck passed, like we had been pulled toward it. And I remember everyone laughing. We all just looked at each other and laughed, and the driver was smiling, and I remember thinking how strange it was."

"You were lucky."

"It always seemed weird to me but natural to start laughing. I guess if you see something enough on television, or whatever, it starts to make sense even if it doesn't. It made sense to me in the van. It was just something we did. We just looked at each other and laughed. And I haven't really thought about it much since then until lately. I remember some of the guys laughing in Afghanistan—they were always laughing, but it was different. They always seemed pissed off, or scared, or embarrassed. It was like they were laughing because they didn't know how to do anything else. I wonder if I'm getting old sometimes, but I know that's not it, because there were, like, fifty-year-old men laughing in that van. And then I think about it, and that moment only lasted for a second. It's just a truck through the windshield, and that's all I see, and then it's gone."

"You never told me that story."

"I guess what I mean is Mom never laughed at the end."

"She did when we first knew each other."

"Sit," he said again, and the dog stood, shifting her eyes, watching the birds. Overhead a shadow passed, a dark triangle on the grass, scattering the crows into the hedges.

"There's that hawk," his father said, and pointed. "Look, Robert."

ACKNOWLEDGMENTS

Many talented writers and editors have offered their time and generosity to this novel—and to my writing and education. My deepest thanks to David M. Olsen, Chih Wang, and the team at Kelp Books, Alexandra Oliva and Elizabeth Boland, Jason Duncan, and the students and instructors of The New School Creative Writing MFA program, particularly Ann Hood, Susan Bell, Stephen Wright, Benjamin Taylor, and my workshop and seminar classmates. Thanks also to Kelly Fordon, Scott Hulet, Jim Newitt, Richard Russo, and Paul Harding.

Special gratitude goes to the Aspen Writers' Workshop, the Community of Writers in the Olympic Valley, the Sewanee Writers' Conference, the Carlisle family, and the Tennessee Williams estate for their support through various workshop and scholarship opportunities.

I'd also like to extend my sincerest thank-you to the writers and journalists whose work offered insight during my research for this novel. Guillermo Cervera's photos from various crisis and conflict zones, as well as his friendship, were illuminating. David J. Morris's exploration of PTSD and generational trauma in *The Evil Hours* was indispensable, as was Tommie Sue Montgomery's *Revolution in El Salvador*, Mark Danner's *The Massacre at El Mozote*, and Renee Montagne and Joanna Kakissis's reporting on the giant Buddha statues in Bamiyan, Afghanistan. I also owe much to and quoted extensively from the United States Marine Corps's *Small Wars Manual* and the United States Army and Marine Corps's *Counterinsurgency Field Manual*. By extension, I'd like to acknowledge those in my family and across the US who have served or continue to serve in the military.

I'd also like to thank Mary and Fred Wilson, Nicolette Howard, Joan Venaglia, Harry Howard, Harry A. Howard, and the Gatto and Setten families. Finally and most importantly, I'd like to thank Laura Gatto Wilson and to express my love and appreciation for her, Juniper, and Clara. The three of you allow me to write with a full heart, always.